I0607838

Abbey Rayne

John Locke

TELEMACHUS PRESS

If you purchased this book without a cover you should be aware that this book is stolen property. It was reported as "unsold and destroyed" to the publisher and neither the author nor the publisher has received any payment for this "stripped book."

This book is a work of fiction. Names, characters, places and incidents are either the product of the author's imagination or are used fictitiously. Any resemblance to actual persons, living or dead, or to actual events or locales is entirely coincidental.

ABBEY RAYNE

Copyright © 2015 John Locke. All rights reserved, including the right to reproduce this book, or portions thereof, in any form. No part of this text may be reproduced, transmitted, downloaded, decompiled, reverse engineered, or stored in or introduced into any information storage and retrieval system, in any form or by any means, whether electronic or mechanical without the express written permission of the author. The scanning, uploading, and distribution of this book via the Internet or via any other means without the permission of the publisher is illegal and punishable by law. Please purchase only authorized electronic editions, and do not participate in or encourage electronic piracy of copyrighted materials.

The publisher does not have any control over and does not assume any responsibility for author or third-party websites or their content.

Cover Designed by: Telemachus Press, LLC
Copyright © Shutterstock/128238230

Visit the author's website:
http://www.donovancreed.com

Published by Telemachus Press, LLC
http://www.telemachuspress.com

ISBN 978-1-942899-72-3 (eBook)
ISBN 978-1-942899-73-0 (paperback)

Version 2015.11.30

10 9 8 7 6 5 4 3 2 1

Medical Warning

Talk to your doctor before beginning a John Locke series, as studies have shown them to be habit-forming and highly addictive. Do not read Locke if you suffer from high blood pressure or other heart-related issues, as readers often experience mood swings, increased pulses, elevated heart rates, and have reported unexpected shifts in body position that take them to the edge of their seats. Do not drive or use machinery while reading Locke novels.

Locke novels are not for everyone, and may cause serious reactions including insomnia, night terrors, and uncontrollable, maniacal laughter. Tell your doctor right away if you have these, or if you experience unusual changes in your behavior including heightened sexual urges, palpitations, or prolonged erections. Common side effects include confusion, hysteria, and trouble swallowing a given premise.

Do not drink alcohol while reading Locke novels, though those with a history of drug or alcohol abuse may be more prone to understanding the material. Adverse reactions to Locke novels include nausea and vomiting, loss of appetite, severe itching, rectal bleeding, purple spots under the skin, and Jimmy Legs. In extreme cases, readers have reported laughing so hard they not only shit their pants, but other's pants, as well. Upon completing a Locke series be prepared to experience symptoms of withdrawal, including fear, anger, extreme sadness, and moderate to severe depression.

Ask your doctor today if John Locke novels are right for you!

Personal Message from John Locke:

I love writing books! But what I love even more is hearing from readers. If you enjoyed this or any of my other books it would mean the world to me if you'd click the link below so you can be on my notification list. That way you can receive updates, contests, prizes, and savings of up to 67% on eBooks immediately after publication!

Just access this link: http://www.DonovanCreed.com, and I'll personally thank you for trying my books.

Also, if you get a chance, I hope you'll check out Dani's website:

http://www.DaniRipper.wordpress.com

John Locke

New York Times Best Selling Author

8th Member of the Kindle Million Sales Club

(Members include James Patterson, George R.R. Martin, and Lee Child)

John Locke had 4 of the top 10 eBooks on Amazon/Kindle at the same time, including #1 and #2!

...Had 6 of the top 20 books at the same time!

...Had 8 books in the top 43 at the same time!

...Has written 30 books in five years in six separate genres, All best-sellers!

...Has been published throughout the world in numerous languages by the world's most prestigious publishing houses!

...Winner, Second Act Magazine's Story of the Year!

...Named by Time Magazine as one of the "Stars of the DIY-Publishing Era"

Wall Street Journal: "John Locke (is) transforming the 'book' business"

John Locke

New York Times Best Selling Author
#1 Best Selling Author on Amazon Kindle

Donovan Creed Series:
Lethal People
Lethal Experiment
Saving Rachel
Now & Then
Wish List
A Girl Like You
Vegas Moon
The Love You Crave
Maybe
Callie's Last Dance
Because We Can!
This Means War!
Boxed In!

Emmett Love Series:
Follow the Stone
Don't Poke the Bear
Emmett & Gentry
Goodbye, Enorma
Rag Soup

Dani Ripper Series:
Call Me!
Promise You Won't Tell?
Teacher, Teacher
Don't Tell Presley!
Abbey Rayne

Dr. Gideon Box Series:
Bad Doctor
Box
Outside the Box
Boxed In!

Other:
Kill Jill
Casting Call

Kindle Worlds:
A Kiss for Luck (Kindle Only)

Non-Fiction:
How I sold 1 Million eBooks in 5 Months!

Dedication:

For my best friend, Sophie Alexander,
Even though she's super mean to me in Chapter 2.
—Love, Dani

Abbey
Rayne

Part One: Dani Ripper

Chapter 1

DOING 70 IN A 35 zone will get you stopped every time.

While the cop runs my license and registration I check my face in the mirror and decide to apply some blush.

How close did I get?

He stopped me just 50 yards from the entrance to the country club where my friend Sarah's bachelorette luncheon has been going on for nearly an hour. I check my watch to confirm.

Make that two hours.

I apply the makeup, return it to my bag, and suddenly see the most horrifying sight you can possibly imagine: I spilled more than a dozen flecks of blush on the crotch and upper thigh of my pants.

My *white* pants.

Shit.

Shit!

I check the console for napkins, and find none.

I try the glove compartment and find...no napkins, but thank God for wet wipes. I remove one from the packet and dab at the tiny spots, hoping somehow they'll magically cling to the cloth without smudging.

Naturally, this doesn't work, and now my pants are smudged.

Hopelessly smudged.

Seriously, I'm sporting a one- by four-inch pink mud mark.

Now my only option is to wipe it vigorously with the wet wipe, so I do, and that removes the blush, but the result is a giant wet spot. I look at myself in the mirror: "Dani, you *idiot*! Can you really be this *stupid*?"

Of course I can. I do this sort of thing all the time.

But what I *can't* do is walk into the country club like this. Sofe will freak.

Sofe (Sophia Renee Alexander, a.k.a. Sophie) is my roommate. Well, she's more than that. If you require full disclosure, I'd have to say she and I...are a couple.

Except for the sex.

I mean, we've *had* sex before, separately *and* together, but...we don't *have* sex. Not very often, anyway. We used to do it more, back when we roll-played, and now that I think about it I bet the role-playing gave me an excuse to do it, since it felt more like a game than real sex, you know? Not that when role-playing we did *everything* two women could possibly do to each other. I mean, for instance we never...uh...

Wait.

I'm giving you *way* too much information, aren't I?

Do me a favor? Forget everything I just said. I can't be responsible for error-free narrative while in full-blown panic over these wet pants.

Speaking of which, this isn't some random, ordinary wet spot. It's more like a lake someone threw my pants into. What I'm saying, there's no way it'll dry on its own for at least an hour.

Think, Dani!

Thankfully, my mind goes to the large wedding card in the gift bag I'm giving Sarah. I retrieve it and start fanning the wet spot as fast and furiously as I can, hoping to speed the drying process. After thirty seconds I check to find it pretty much unchanged.

If only I had a napkin or towel...but I don't. So I redouble my effort, and fan myself even harder, like my life's at stake. Back and forth, faster, faster, till I'm fanning so hard I don't even hear the cop approach the open window till he says, "I knew you were smokin' hot when I pulled you over, so I'm not surprised you have to fan your pussy to keep it from bursting into flames!"

Huh? What the...

I'm so outraged it takes a moment to form the words. When I've got them I look into his grinning face and say, "That's the most disgusting and vulgar thing anyone has ever said to me."

He looks me over. "That can't possibly be true."

I think a moment. "Well, maybe not. But it's the worst thing a policeman ever said."

"I might give you that. But you know what I think?"

"No. And I couldn't care less."

"I think you like it when guys talk dirty to you. Especially cops."

My eyes go wide. "That does it!"

He laughs. "What're you gonna do, report me?"

"Don't think I won't!"

"How about I tear up the ticket and we call it even?"

I pause. Should I? Normally I'd consider that a fair trade. But there's something seriously wrong with this guy, and I'd feel awful if he wound up hurting someone. So I grab a pen and notebook from the console and prepare to write, but can't find a number on his badge.

"What's your name?"

"Jack Inghoff."

I write it down. "Badge number?"

"Sixty-nine."

I start to write, then frown. Then glance at the name I wrote and frown deeper. Jack Inghoff? Jacking Off? Badge 69? I show him angry eyes. "You think this is *funny?* What the hell kind of cop *are* you?"

"A fake one."

For a second, I'm terrified. Then he says, "Relax, Dani. I'm a stripper. They hired me for the same bachelorette party you're going to. Except that unlike you, I'm *supposed* to be late."

You might wonder how he knows I'm going to the party.

Simple.

Upon approaching my car his first question was: "Where you headin' in such a rush?" I told him, and tried to talk him out of giving me a ticket, but he was having none of it. And now I learn he's a fucking stripper.

"You deliberately wasted my time."

"You mad, bro?"

"You took my license and registration!"

"Sure did, sweet thing."

I feel my face boiling with anger. "Why?"

"I like you. It's the only way I could think to get your name and address."

"That's stalking!"

"Not *yet*, it isn't."

I glance in the mirror, see the flashing lights.

"You're driving a *cop* car!"

"No I'm not. It's just a sedan, with a flashing light I stick on the roof when I get to whatever venue I'm performing."

"I could have you arrested for this."

"It'd be your word against mine."

He's right. But that doesn't mean I can't tell him what I think: "You're a dick!"

He grins. "Ouch."

"Give me back my license!"

He hands me the registration, but says, "I'll return your license after my performance. By the way, you're gonna *love* it!"

"I won't give you a second look."

"You won't *have* to, sweet thing. After the first look, you won't be able to turn away. Then, later on, I'll show you a better way to cool down that pussy."

With that, he turns and heads to his car.

I'm appalled, outraged, seething with fury...but power-less to do anything about it, so I honk my horn and scream the full string of cusswords I've heard in my life, even the ones whose meanings I don't know—and am surprised how short the list is. Then I realize it's even shorter, since I dou-bled up on *fuck-faced shit bastard*. I pause to think of any vile words I might have omitted, and come up with "Queefing pondscum!" which I yell, even while realizing it makes no sense. So I cover that mistake by yelling "*You...*" I toss in two adjectives in search of a noun: "*dick-farting...*" but then won-der if those might actually be adverbs, and...by the time I think of a noun: "*whore!*" I've totally lost the moment.

He laughs, bends over, shakes his ass at me.

I immediately resolve to do two things: learn more cusswords, and practice using them in real-life situations.

I grip my steering wheel hard as I can and fume in si-lence. Then surprise myself by letting out a loud, frustrated shriek, after which I take a deep breath, look in the mirror, and try to determine how long it will take to go from *this*...to fun and perky.

Chapter 2

NOW, ENTERING THE PACKED ROOM, I find myself apologizing profusely to everyone I encounter as I make my way to Sophie's table. When I get there her icy stare tells me she's angrier than Donald Trump at a Megyn Kelly tribute dinner. I take my seat beside her and try to hold her hand, but she pulls away. I whisper I'm sorry, and at first she won't even look at me, but then she finally *does* turn to say something, only to be interrupted by Sarah's sudden announcement over the PA system:

"Ladies? Who's ready to play *The Best Friend's Game?*"

Everyone is.

Sarah asks for volunteers, and I see Sofe looking straight into my eyes.

I shake my head no.

She smiles, but not in a good way.

The Best Friend's Game is like *Truth or Dare* on steroids. Sofe knows how much I hate this game, but she's pissed and thrilled: pissed at me for being two hours late, and thrilled for the opportunity to exact her revenge. She jumps to her feet and offers us up as contestants. Everyone loves the idea, and why wouldn't they? Straight women love hearing the intimate details of two young ladies who are...exploring their sexuality.

I try to back out, but Sofe says, "Come on, Dani, be a sport. It's the *least* you can do for being so late. And anyway, it'll be great fun!"

The gleam in her eye tells me fun's the last thing this is gonna be.

Of course, all the women and girls in the room start chanting "Dani! Dani!" to make it impossible for me to say no.

So here we are, ten minutes into the game, and of course we're killing it, since not only are we super close, but Sofe is also monstrously competitive, and hedging her bet by airing all our personal secrets.

Want an example?

Sarah asked, "Which of you is more naïve? And give us an example to prove your point." We both agreed I was the naïve one. Then Sofe said, "One morning Dani woke up screaming, 'Omigod! My *hands*! My *hands*! Are they *huge*?'"

Then she explained, "Dani had bought boob cream to make her boobs bigger. She rubbed it all over her chest, then went to bed and woke up thinking if the cream worked, it might make her hands bigger, too!"

Of course, everyone thought that was hilarious, and I just closed my eyes and hoped if I couldn't see them, they might not be able to see me. I soldiered on, knowing we were close to the end of the game. Honestly, angry as Sofe was, I'm surprised she didn't burn me worse.

Which brings us to present time.

Sarah says, "This is a two-part question, worth 20 points. I'll direct my question to Sophie, who's turned out to be the life of the party. Sophie, if you get both questions right you and Dani win the game. Are you ready?"

Sofe's so excited she starts dancing like Ickey Woods getting cold cuts at the grocery. "Let's do it!" she says.

"Okay, here goes. Question number one: what is your best friend's favorite sex toy?"

The place goes wild. Picture 60 straight women and girls gasping with shock, howling with laughter.

Sarah adds, "Feel free to give a brand name or detailed description."

"Sofe?" I say, with pleading eyes.

She shows me a radiant smile filled with malice. If that sounds contradictory, you don't know Sofe.

I go for broke and give her my most severe warning look so she'll know not to divulge such personal information to a roomful of nosey, gossipy women for no higher purpose than to beat three other best friends who got roped into playing this appalling game.

But the combination of (a) wanting to punish me for being late and (b) imminent victory proves too powerful, and so she says, "Dani indeed has a favorite sex toy. And it's called the *Vibrating Clit Flogger!*"

I recoil in horror, squeeze my mortified eyes shut, and feel the red creeping up my neck as 60 females—some of whom are *teenagers*—come unglued with delight.

There's no point denying the *Clit Flogger*. After all, this isn't *The Newlywed Game*, where you have to predict what your significant other has written on a card. No, this game is designed to elicit the most intimate secrets between friends. And the reason we're winning is because the other best friends refuse to answer the toughest questions, believing—as I do—there are certain things the whole world doesn't need to know. I mean, if I wanted people to know I've pleasured myself with a *Vibrating Clit Flogger* I'd write a book.

When the laughter *finally* dies down, Sarah looks at her question card and reads, "For the victory and the trophy, here's the second part of your question: where does your best friend hide her favorite sex toy?"

As all eyes stare at me, hoping to learn what is possibly the last sexual secret Sophie hasn't revealed, I can finally relax. There's no way she knows where I hide my *Vibrating Clit Flogger*.

But Sofe flashes me an evil grin, then turns to face the room and—I shit you not—she actually stands and clears her throat. "You are not going to *believe* this!" she says, as if the information she's about to impart will eclipse the discovery of the DNA double helix.

"Sofe?" I plead. "Please don't do this."

But does she even look in my direction?

No.

She says, for all the world to hear: "Dani has no idea I know this, but she hides her *Vibrating Clit Flogger* in the bottom of a box she keeps in the upstairs closet. The box is filled with her photos and scrapbooks, but has *my* name on it. Will someone please ask why she put *my* name on the box?"

Everyone yells, "Why did she put *your* name on the box?"

And Sofe says, "Because if she happens to die and someone finds her *Vibrating Clit Flogger* while searching through her personal effects, they'll think it belongs to *me!*"

Furious, I finally snap, yelling, "Do you think you can say *Vibrating Clit Flogger* one more time? You know, just in case Sarah's great grandmother didn't happen to hear you the first 20?"

As if on cue, a withered voice from the back of the room says, "I heard it just fine, dear!"

Sofe says, "Actually, the *Vibrating Clit Flogger* was designed to be worn by a man, to stimulate his female partner. But as Dani continues to prove, the *Vibrating Clit Flogger* can be used solo."

And that's when it hits me: she's not just punishing me for being late, she's also punishing me because we haven't been having sex. Not only that, but I think she's jealous of Spin.

Um...I meant to say...my vibrator. So anyway...

Well, this is awkward. I didn't mean to say that, but...yeah, I named my vibrator. To—you know, make her—*it!*—seem less impersonal.

It's not like I'm calling out, "Oh, Spin! Omigod! Yes, YES!" or anything like that when I'm in the throes of...

Whoa.

How about we just do what we did earlier: forget this part and move along. Will that work for you?

Good.

Thank you.

And please. *PLEASE!* Don't tell Sofe about Spin, okay? Because that would be the final nail in our relationship coffin, assuming she takes it the wrong way, which she will...unless she doesn't.

What I'm trying to say, Sofe's a woman. I mean, I'm a woman too, but she's the only woman I've ever lived with, and maybe we're all like this and I never knew it before, but I never have the slightest clue how Sofe will construe whatever I say or do.

Personally, I think the three hardest things in the world to predict are jury decisions; what aging rock stars will sleep with; and how the woman you love will react to your most innocent action or comment. Because only a woman can feed the rose blossoms of your heart through the meat grinder of her brain and extrude the foulest sausage.

So please don't tell Sofe...or anyone else about this whole Spin thing. It can be our little secret, okay?

Thank you. And yes, you can tell me your secrets, and I'll keep them safe.

Fair enough?

Okay then.

You probably want to know what's going on at the party in real time: apparently Sofe has noticed the look on my face, or the tears streaming down it, because it finally seems to have dawned on her what she's done. The amount of damage.

She says, "Dani, I—"

"It's okay," I say. "I deserved it. I'm sorry for being late. Sorry for not having more sex. Sorry for...whatever else I've done."

"I love you!" she says, and if things had stopped right there we probably would've been fine. But suddenly the lights dimmed and the room filled with the shrill sound of a whistle, and...

The fake cop arrived and started yelling for the guest of honor.

I'll make this part short: after jumping, gyrating, and stripping down to his thong, the fake cop gave our mortified friend Sarah a lap dance that included straddling her thigh and grinding his manhood against it the same way my Uncle Teddy's sex-starved dog does after catching a whiff of estrogen. Except he did it so violently it reminded me of a bushman I saw on the Discovery channel who tried to kill a snake by repeatedly slamming it into a rock. The women are howling, but Sarah's thoroughly grossed out, as are her future in-laws.

Of course, the reprehensible highlight occurs when the stripper dares Sarah to reach into his thong for a "special surprise." She declines, but a champagne-sotted soccer mom takes him up on his challenge, and grabs his cock.

"Ow!" He screams. "That's *not* the surprise!"

With great effort he extracts her determined hand from his quickly diminishing asset, then hands Sarah the small rectangular card that turns out to be my driver's license. Leaving the entire room—and especially Sofe—to wonder how my driver's license ended up in his dick sling.

Bad as this is, it's about to get worse as we hear voices from outside the room. Apparently the stripper forgot to turn off his mike when he left, and the whole room can hear him telling someone: "Yeah, that's right. Two hundred bucks for ten minutes of work. Plus driving time. Not bad, but I'd trade it right now for a shot of whiskey and a blow job from Dani Ripper."

I instinctively jump to my feet and run full speed toward the door to tell him to turn off his mike, but Sarah's great grandmother shouts, "Don't forget the shot of whiskey!"

I stop in my tracks and look at Sofe like a deer caught in headlights.

Sarah walks to our table, places my driver's license into my water glass, shoots me a withering look and says, "Well, I guess we all know why Dani was late to the party."

There is no laughter in the room, nor a single smile.

The silence is deafening.

Before walking away, Sarah mouths the word *Asshole* at me.

Finally, mercifully, Sofe stands, retrieves my driver's license, dries it with a napkin, then smiles and says, "Well, *this* was certainly fun! Can't wait to see you all at the wedding!" She looks at me. "Ready to go, Dani?"

I nod.

Chapter 3

AFTER A FROSTY WEEKEND with Sofe, and 270,000 YouTube hits, and the announcement of record sales by the company that manufactures the *Vibrating Clit Flogger*, I've become more popular than *Astro Glide* at a circle jerk. But that was then, and this morning I'm past it and happy to be sitting in my office with Margaret Thatcher (my client, not the former Prime Minister), who's about to tell me how my private investigative firm can give her a more fulfilling life (her words, not mine). So far the only things I know about Margaret is she perspires profusely and has an annoying habit of sniffing enthusiastically after uttering each sentence:

"I checked you out online." *Sniff!* "And was shocked at what I found." *Sniff!*

I hold my hands up in protest. "I was young. I needed the money!"

"Excuse me?" *Sniff!*

"Uh...never mind. What did you find that shocked you?"

"You're the Little Girl Who Got Away!" *Sniff!*

I sigh. "Yes, much as I hate backstory, I am indeed the famously kidnapped teen who was held prisoner by a psychotic rapist ten years ago. How can I help you?"

"I want you to investigate my husband." *Sniff!*

"You think he's cheating on you?"

"No, of course not!" *Sniff!*

I cock my head. "Well, this is unusual. What's he done?"

"Nothing, far as I know." *Sniff!* "He's as honest as the day is long." *Sniff!*

"Summer or winter?"

Margaret's look indicates she's confused, so I say: "This past Father's Day, June 21st, was the longest day of the year: 14 hours and 31 minutes. But last year, December 21st was the shortest. Here in Nashville we only had 9 hours, 49 minutes and 43 seconds of daylight. What I'm asking, is your husband as honest as June 21st or December 21st?"

"You're an odd duck," she says.

I wait for the sniff.

No sniff.

"Quack," I say.

No response.

It takes me a full minute to realize Margaret Thatcher has died.

Now, an hour later, the police aren't buying my story. One says, "You expect me to believe she was just sitting here, talking normally, and died without making a sound?"

"No sir."

"Then tell me what happened."

"I just did."

"What do you mean?"

"I told you what happened. You asked if I expected you to believe it, and I said no. But that's what happened."

He gives me a curious look, and starts to speak, but I interrupt him: "Don't say I'm an odd duck."

"Why not?"

"Because that's what *she* said. And *now* look at her!"

Chapter 4

THE INVESTIGATION INTO MARGARET Thatcher's untimely death takes time and draws so many people I'm forced to reschedule my "Labor of Love" client to 3 p.m.

After telling my story for the third time the detectives finally allow me to leave. I drive straight home to get a hug from Sofe, but she's not home, so I try to think of something to do to pass the time and...I know exactly what you're thinking:

This would be the perfect time to break out my *Vibrating Clit Flogger*, right?

No way!

Much as I'd like to, I know a setup when I see one: here's Dani, all alone in the house, moaning and groaning right up to the moment Sophie and 6 priests, 12 nuns, and 3 bishops burst into the room as I'm shouting, "Oh God! Oh God! YES!"

Reality check: to the best of my knowledge Sofe doesn't know a single priest, nun, or bishop. No matter. I guarantee you the minute I reach for Spin, that very gang will put my bedroom on their parade route.

For this reason—and because Margaret Thatcher died in my office a couple hours ago—I ignore my friend in the upstairs bedroom closet and choose instead to make some tea and watch Maury Povich reruns hoping to learn some dance moves from the guys who just found out they are NOT the father. I love how Maury keeps a straight face through all these shows and never makes moral judgments. He's always calm, cheerful, reassuring, and confident: "Don't worry, we'll find your baby's father. We're getting so close! We've only tested 14 men so far, which only leaves 86 other possibilities." Since his guests and my clients share the same genetic profiles, I study Maury like a hawk. He's to me like St. Augustine is to a divinity student.

11 a.m. comes and goes, so I call Sofe and tell her about Margaret Thatcher.

She says, "Wow, right in your office? That's creepy. I mean, terrible, of course, but...creepy, too." She pauses, then says, "How are you handling it? Should we meet for lunch or go shoe-shopping?"

"Good question. I didn't really know her, so...lunch should do the trick. Where are you?"

"Daphne's."

"Oh. Right." I forgot she finally worked up the nerve to visit her sister. "How's it going?"

"I'll tell you at lunch. You feel like Alexanders?"

"How could I not? It's your surname, after all! But do me a quick favor and Face-Time me."

"Why?"

"I need you to tell me how I look."

"Where are you?"

"Home. In the master bath."

"There's a mirror right there."

"I never look in mirrors when I'm alone in the house."

"Is this a joke?"

"Nope."

"You can't be serious."

"Pretend I am."

"Okay. Let's hear it."

"In the movies when you're home alone and look in the mirror you always see the killer in the reflection—"

She sighs.

—"or a vampire."

It takes 15 minutes to drive to Alexanders, and twice that to secure a table. Now that we're seated, Sofe starts by asking, "Was that her real name or is that what we're calling her?"

"Margaret Thatcher? Yeah, that's her real name."

"Highly unusual, don't you think?"

"Not really. Highly unusual is like when I found those human tonsils on our doorstep, or like when Fanny shows up for work. Margaret Thatcher's a pretty common name."

"Actually, I was talking about how she happened to die right in the middle of talking to you."

"Oh. Right."

Sofe laughs. "Ever notice how many weird clients you get?"

"Well technically, Margaret wasn't a client."

"I know, but still."

"I think it has to do with my advertising."

She smiles. "No Case Too Small?"

I nod. Then say, "You know what I need?"

"A psychiatrist?"

"A new slogan. Something that says *Dani*. It'll be cute, catchy, and perfect. And when everyone sees it they'll say, 'Omigod! Only Dani could have thought of that!'"

"Got any ideas?"

"I was thinking you could come up with something."

She laughs. "*That's* what sounds like Dani! When do you get your office back?"

"One o'clock. Good thing too, since this is shaping up to be a record day for me."

"New clients?"

"Two, plus my Labor of Love."

"Uh...refresh me on that."

"The football player? Sweet Pea Johnson?"

She thinks a minute, then shakes her head. "Sorry."

"Lady hired us to find old high school film footage on her husband?"

Sofe nods. "Got it! That was forever ago."

"Wasn't easy, but today's the day. They're coming at three. Want to join us?"

She bites her lip. "Uh...do you *want* me there?"

"Of course! If you're available."

"Then it's settled: no way!"

She laughs to show she's kidding, and I say, "You're a good friend, Sofe. Much better to me than I am to you."

"I know, but tell me why."

"You're always there for me."

"True. What else?"

The waitress appears, takes our iced tea order. When she leaves I ask, "How'd it go with Daphne?"

"Scandalously!"

I raise an eyebrow. "That sounds interesting! Spill it!"

"Daphne wasn't home. She actually has a *job*, if you can believe it. But that's not the big news. Brace yourself: I caught my niece smoking a joint."

"Omigod! *Gwennie?*"

"Uh huh."

"How *old* is she?"

"Sixteen. Barely!"

"*Jesus*, Sofe! What'd you *do?*"

"Took a deep breath, asked her how long this had been going on, and asked if she'd be willing to let me talk to her about drugs. Know what she said? 'Absolutely! What type of drugs are you looking for, Aunt Sophie?' Can you *believe* it?"

I laugh. "And you said?"

"I didn't know *what* to say. But when she told me how little she charges for X, I totally freaked! Now I'm her best customer."

"You're joking, right?"

She shrugs.

"Sofe? That was a joke, right?"

The waitress brings our drinks and says, "Have you looked at the menus?"

We tell her we have.

"Then without further ado," she says, "let me tell you our lunch specials."

She does, and we make our choices. After she leaves I say, "Did you hear that?"

"What?"

"Our waitress said, 'Without further ado.'"

"So?"

"What's ado?"

Sofe rolls her eyes. "Do me a favor, okay? Don't start this crap right now."

"I'm serious, Sofe. I honestly don't know."

She eyes me carefully. "It means no more chitchat. She was getting straight to the point."

"I understand *how* she meant it, I'm just wondering what it *is*."

"You should spend more time wondering how you got insane."

"It's a simple question."

"Ado means no more talk."

"Yes. But doesn't it also mean no further delays?"

She sighs. "I suppose."

"If it means both those things, why not say 'without further talk or delay?'"

"Who cares?"

"I do! I want to know how *ado* came to mean those things, and why people say it."

The lady sitting at the table beside us says, "I can't *stand* it anymore! Do you *ever* shut up? You should thank God people still say ado."

I look at Sofe like, "Whaaa?" But the lady continues: "I'm Chloe Kincaid, professor emerita, linguistics, University of Cambridge, United Kingdom. And you are?"

"Um...Dani Ripper?"

"You sound unsure. Either you *are* Dani Ripper, or you're not. Which is it?"

"I am."

"Very well, I'll take you at your word. So: Ms. Ripper."

"Yes?"

"I couldn't help but overhear your conversation, and you'll be pleased to know I have the undisputed answer to your question: *without further ado* is an idiom that represents one of the few surviving uses of the noun *ado*, which literally means, 'what is being done.'"

I widen my eyes at Sofe, but she's speechless. Not knowing what else to do, I tell the lady, "Thank you."

"Not so fast!" she says. "Centuries ago it was widely used. Case in point, Shakespeare's delightful comedy, *Much Ado about Nothing*, which was written toward the middle of the Bard's career, during the years 1598 and 99. Do you understand what I'm saying?"

"Not really."

She frowns. "I'm saying you should be thankful this phrase endures in our language, because when it's gone, the word *ado* will be extinct. That cannot be allowed to happen, understood? Now finish your lunch."

"Yes ma'am."

With that, Professor Kincaid pays her bill, stands, and walks away. I'm about to say, "Can you believe that?" But before I get a chance, her empty seat is claimed by an oddly-dressed man whose crazy eyes immediately find a home in my cleavage. I try to ignore him, but he's making it impossible.

I show him a deep frown and say, "Do you *mind?*"

He doesn't seem to, and continues to stare, so I stare back. He's wearing a red-and-white striped t-shirt and red shorts and looks like Pugsley from the old *Addams Family* TV show, except that he's in his late 40's.

"Your menu's on the table, not in my blouse" I say, loudly enough to publicly embarrass him. But Pugsley's not embarrassed in the least. The fact I'm paying attention to him gives him the confidence to say: "Did you know girls can have babies?"

Sofe giggles.

Realizing he's a special needs person, I panic and go politically incorrect, meaning I look away, then down at my food and pretend I didn't hear him. But he raises his voice and says, "You're girls."

"That's right," Sofe says, encouraging him. "What's your name?"

"Bobby."

"Are you here by yourself?" she says.

"Girls can have babies," Bobby says. "Boys can't."

"Right again," Sofe says. "Who taught you that?"

"My mom."

He reverts to his comfort zone: staring at my boobs.

Sofe grins at me.

Bobby says, "Girls have boobies and vaginas."

Sofe says, "Dani? Feel free to join in any time."

I keep my head down, say nothing.

Bobby says, "Boobies look like fried eggs."

Sofe bursts out laughing and says, "Fried *eggs?*"

I frown at her.

Bobby says, "Uh huh. I've *seen* them before."

Sofe says, "Whose boobies have you seen, Bobby?"

"My mom's."

Sofe nods. "That explains a lot."

I give her a look.

Bobby says, "Girls make pee pee from their vaginas and poopy from their butts."

Sofe pretends to look confused and says, "I'm not sure. Is that right, Dani?"

I give her a stern look and mouth, *Shut. Up!*

She laughs.

Bobby says, "Babies grow in your tummy and come out your—"

"Actually, we're *women*," I say, interrupting him. "Not girls."

He looks confused a moment, then says, "Women can have babies too."

"That's right," Sofe says. Then adds, "I'm Sophie and this is my friend, Dani. What's your full name?"

"Bobby Wartman."

"Nice to meet you, Bobby. Are you here by yourself?"

"Yes. I drove here all by myself."

"On your bicycle?"

"No. My truck."

"You have a *driver's* license?"

"Yes. And I like soup."

"What kind of soup?"

"The hot kind."

Sofe and I look at each other.

Bobby says, "I have a girlfriend."

Sofe says, "Does *she* know it?"

"Yes."

"What's her name?"

"Eleanor."

"That's a nice name."

"Yes. But I call her Mom."

"Is that because she's nice to you?"

"No. It's because she's my mom."

"Ah."

He says, "Did you know girls can make doo doo?"

I try to make eye contact with a passing waitress, but she ignores me, so I holler, "*Check please!*" She continues to ignore me, so I get to my feet and start searching for our actual waitress. I find her, pay the bill, and motion Sofe to meet me in the lobby. When she does I say, "I can't believe you sat there and talked to that guy."

"I felt sorry for him."

"He shouldn't be driving. He needs a keeper."

"I agree."

"You were with him almost five minutes. What did you talk about, doo doo?"

"Among other things. By the way, he makes the long, stinky kind."

"Omigod! He *told* you that?"

"He did."

"I bet his driver's license is written in crayon."

"Actually, it's real. He showed it to me."

I purse my lips. "I'm calling bullshit on that."

"It's a valid Tennessee driver's license. Swear to God."

"You've seen it."

"I have."

"And he drives a car."

"Truck."

"Right. Of course. And did he show you his pee pee?"

She laughs.

I say, "What else did you talk about?"

"His job."

"He has a *job*?"

"He does."

"Bless someone's heart."

"What do you mean?"

"I can't imagine having the patience to hire a person like that. Oh wait. It's probably his mother. The one whose boobies look like fried eggs!"

Sofe and I hold it for a second, then burst out laughing. Then she says, "He likes you."

"He likes my boobs, you mean. Jesus, Sofe, I can't believe you told him our *names*!"

"Sorry."

"What does he do?"

"You mean his job?"

"Yeah."

"Prime example."

"Of what?"

"Your tax dollars at work."

"What do you mean?"

"He's an FBI agent."

I give her a look. "No shit?"

"Swear to God."

I think about it a minute, then nod. "Makes sense."

"How so?"

"I heard they were upgrading."

Chapter 5

MY FIRST CLIENT OF the afternoon, Vicki Yetti, wants me to find a man's cell phone number. She has his home number, but every time she calls, his wife answers.

"Who's the man?"

"My old college boyfriend."

"Does he know you're trying to call?"

"No, but I expect he'll be thrilled to hear from me." She pauses. "Are you going to give me a lecture about why I should leave him alone?"

Normally I would. But then I ask myself *What would Maury do?*—and answer: "No. If I start lecturing clients about the poor choices they make, I'd go broke in no time."

"So you'll help me?"

"Yes, absolutely." *Don't worry, Vicki. I'll find your baby's daddy!*

I knock on the wall behind me, and seconds later Dillon enters my office. Dillon's my teenaged, computer genius partner. I tell him what we need, and he asks for the old boyfriend's name and address. Vicki doesn't know the address, but gives him the name and home phone number. Five minutes later he comes back in and hands me a slip of paper.

"This is it?" I say.

He nods.

I hand it to Vicki, saying, "I hope things work out for the best."

She looks at the number. "How much do I owe you?"

"Fifty."

"*Dollars?*"

"Yup."

"That's insane!"

"Too little?"

"Too much!"

"You think fifty dollars is too much to secure your future happiness?"

"It's just a phone number. The happiness is up to me."

"Still, without the number..."

"It took you five *minutes!*"

"Should we have made you wait two hours, like other detective agencies would have done?"

"Doesn't matter. I'm not paying you fifty dollars."

Vicki has turned out to be as charming as gut yeast.

I sigh. "What do *you* feel it's worth?"

"Nothing. And that's exactly what I'm paying you."

"We solved your case," I say. "We deserve to be paid."

She gets up to leave. "Sorry. I never signed a contract."

I smack my head. "You're right. Please remember that, later on."

She cocks her head. "What do you mean?"

"If you're unhappy with the results, remember those two things: we never signed a contract, and you refused to pay us."

"No problem. Have a nice life."

"You too."

It takes five minutes for my phone to ring. When it does, I smile at Dillon, put the phone on speaker and say, "Hi Vicki!"

She sputters, "Wh-what the *fuck?*"

"This isn't our first rodeo. Dillon has your old boyfriend's cell number. But the new price is $100."

"That's bullshit!"

"I agree, but those are my terms."

She can't see me smiling, but Dillon can, and it feels good to finally stick up for myself.

Vicki sneers, "I'll get the number from one of your competitors."

"Fine. But they'll charge you $200, and make you wait at *least* two hours."

"I'll give you a horrible review on Yelp."

"Big deal. You think I'm afraid of you? I've stared *death* in the eye. And anyway, I'll respond to your review by saying we couldn't help you because you refused to sign a contract. Best wishes, thanks for stopping by."

I hang up the phone and say, "Now we wait."

Dillon says, "You've stared *death* in the eye?"

"Yup."

34

"What does that even mean?"

I shrug. "I have no idea, but I've said it at least twenty times, and you're the first person who ever asked me about it."

"You probably saw it on TV."

"You can't prove that."

Moments later, Fanny buzzes me and says, "I might be knocked up."

"There's a shock. Anything else?"

"Vicki Yetti's in the lobby. She wants the phone number."

I smile at Dillon. "Send her back."

"She refuses to see you."

"Did she give you $100?"

"She did."

"Check or cash?"

"Check."

"Tell her it has to be cash."

I listen as she does, and hear Vicki scream, "Fuck *you*, Dani Ripper!"

In the end, no one fucked anyone. She coughed up the cash, Dillon gave her the number, and I used the time between appointments to study last month's profit and loss statement, which brings us to the present, where Fanny escorts the next client into my office, introduces him as Merle, and asks, "Can I stay?"

"Why?"

"I want to see the look on your face when Merle tells you his problem."

Merle says, "I don't mind."

35

I shrug, offer him a seat, then walk back around my desk. Before I get a chance to sit, Merle says, "Wait. That chair!"

"What about it?"

"Is that a Skape Highback?"

I smile. "You like it?"

He says, "I've never seen one in person. They're like, $6,500, right?"

"Six thousand, eight hundred and twenty-five, to be exact."

Fanny says, "You're probably wondering why she's placed a $10 desk in front of it."

"Well, it is a bit incongruous."

"It was a gift," I say.

"Wow!" he says. "I must be doing something wrong. My big gift this year was a Weed Wacker."

"Always useful," Fanny says.

"Except that I live in a high rise apartment. No grass."

"Actually, I was referring to man-scaping," she says.

They're both right about the chair being completely out of place in my two-bit office. But I don't dare throw it away, since it was given by a crime lord, after learning one of my clients murdered his former associate in Witness Protection.

As I study Merle's face and eye trajectory it dawns on me he might be using the chair as an excuse to stare at my boobs. Sofe says I have tit fixation, and constantly think men are staring at my boobs. She says it's common for those with smaller chests to subconsciously think men are judging them negatively. My take is that men regard boobs in a blouse like kids regard toys in a toy store. Size doesn't matter. They want to *see* the toys; touch them, play with them. It's just that I'm not as comfortable sharing my toys as others are. In Merle's case, he can't see the chair with me sitting in it, so what else could he possibly be looking at if not my boobs? Not that there's much to see. Like Sofe says, I'm not super endowed, or anything. Of course, some guys like girls with smaller...

"Before you sat down," Merle says, "did I see a bullet hole in the head rest?"

"We think so," Fanny says.

Actually we *know* so. The crime boss's gift came with a warning of what to expect if I ever cross him. I thanked him for giving me the message with a chair instead of a puppy. Bullet hole aside, I still think Merle's checking out my cherry stones.

"What can I do for you, Merle?"

"I want you to follow my wife."

"What's her name?"

"Janie."

"You think she's cheating on you?"

"Of course not. But she might be taking illicit drugs."

"What makes you think that?"

"She's having hallucinations, but refuses to see a doctor."

"Can you give me an example?"

"A couple nights ago we were in bed, and she started crying and said she was having hallucinations."

"You remember her exact words?"

"Yes. She said, 'Merle, I have to tell you something. I've been seeing someone else.' I said, 'Another man?' and she said 'Yes.' I said, 'You mean right now?' and she said, 'Yes. But it's been going on for months.'"

I cock my head.

Merle says, "At first I thought she was kidding. But she said she's seen him everywhere: at her office, in hotel rooms, and even in our bedroom while I was at work. I asked, 'Who is it?' and she said, 'Don't worry, it's not someone you know. I'm so sorry.' Can you imagine?"

"I...No. I mean, I'm not sure. What happened next?"

"Well, I told her this is completely unacceptable, and insisted she see a neurologist. What's wrong?"

"I'm looking for the camera."

"What camera?"

"Fanny? I'm being punked, right?"

She laughs. "If you *are*, no one told *me*."

I look at Merle. "This is a joke, right?"

"Why would I joke about my wife being a drug addict?"

"I truly don't know."

He says, "I did some online research and learned that certain illicit drugs can alter a person's perception of reality and make them think they're seeing things. Since Janie's refusing to see a doctor, I have to assume she's taking LSD, peyote, psilocybin, or—God help her—PCP."

"This is what you have to assume?"

"Do you have a better explanation?"

"Yes. She's cheating on you."

He frowns. "That's ridiculous." He sighs. "Look, Ms. Ripper, I don't expect you to understand the type of relationship Janie and I have, but we've always been completely honest with each other. If she's cheating on me, she'd say so."

"Just for the sake of argument, how could she say it in way that's so obvious you'd accept it?"

"She'd have to say, 'I'm cheating on you with another man.'"

"And you'd accept that?"

"Yes, of course."

I nod. "How much are you prepared to pay me to figure out if your wife is taking hallucinogenic drugs?"

"Whatever it costs."

"Would you pay me a thousand dollars?"

"Yes."

"I'll do it for a hundred."

His eyes go wide. "Seriously?"

"Yup. One hundred. Up front. In cash."

He reaches into his pocket, pulls out a wad of cash, peels off five twenties, and hands them to me. I place the cash in an envelope, seal it, and place it in the slot behind my desk, knowing it'll slide through the wall into Dillon's eager, greedy hands.

"Let's get her on the phone," I say.

When she answers I say, "Janie, I'm Dani Ripper. I'm a friend of your husband's."

"Oh really? How long has *this* been going on?"

"Just a few minutes."

"I see. And do you plan on seeing him again?"

"I'm not sure. Probably not."

"I don't blame you in the least."

I say, "Merle told me you've been seeing someone else."

"Is that why he went to see *you?*"

"Yes."

"Should I assume you're going to charge him for the visit?"

"Yes."

"How much?"

"He offered a thousand, but I'm only charging him a hundred."

She sighs. "Poor Merle." Then she adds, "What do you want from me?"

"I'd like to ask you a question."

"Can I ask you something first?"

"Of course."

"Why would I want to talk to a hooker?"

"I have no idea. Wait. Is this a riddle? Does the hooker live in the North Pole?"

"Are you insane?"

"I'm in Nashville."

Janie pauses. Then says, "Actually, you seem a perfect match for my husband."

"Thank you."

"I suppose you have lots of other clients."

"Not as many as I'd like."

"How many, altogether?"

Wow, she's nosey! But it's not *that* big a deal. So I say, "I'd have to check my records, but I'd guess around two hundred."

"*Seriously?* Two hundred *clients?*"

"Give or take."

"How can you *possibly* service that many?"

"I have a partner."

"Just *one?* Holy crap!"

"And a secretary."

"Still! You guys must be working day and night, 24/7!"

"We're pretty dedicated."

"I'll say!"

"Ready for my questions?"

"Go ahead. I feel I've taken up a lot of your time already."

"Merle thinks you're using hallucinogenic drugs, but I think you're simply cheating on him. Are you in fact having sex with another man?"

"No."

"Told you!" Merle says.

Janie says, "I'm having sex with *lots* of other men."

"Told you!" I say to Merle. Then realize I could have gloated in a more professional way. When he leaves, I lean back in my insanely expensive chair, close my eyes, and wonder why anyone would want to do this for a living.

Minutes later, Fanny buzzes me: "Got time for a walk-in? Her name's Hester Darrow."

"By all means, send her back. Wow, so many clients today! I feel like quite the squirrel with all these nuts you keep sending me!"

A woman's voice says, "I heard that!"

"Oops!" Fanny says. "Forgot I put you on speaker."

Chapter 6

"MS. RIPPER?"

"Yes?"

"I'm Hester Darrow. I didn't appreciate that remark."

"I'm sorry. It's just been one of those days, you know?"

"I do not."

"Well, that's good, I suppose. Anyway, it's nice to meet you, Hester. How'd you find me?"

"What do you mean? Were you missing?"

"No."

"Hiding?

"No. I was basically asking if someone recommended me, or if you saw my ad in the paper, or—"

"Neither," she says. "The police mentioned your name and I wrote it down."

I smile. "Then it *was* a recommendation."

"I wouldn't call it that. They told me to stop wasting their time. Said if I kept bothering Mr. Chambers he was going to take out a restraining order on me, so I asked if they knew any private detectives I could talk to, and they laughed. Can you believe it? They *laughed* at me! Then one of them said, 'She should call Dani Ripper!' Then he said, 'Wah! I broke my nail!' And the other detective said, 'Do handcuffs only come in silver? That's so last year!' and they laughed some more."

"Lovely. Anything else?"

"They said you were highly effable, but I couldn't find that word in the dictionary. What's it mean?"

It means they think I'm highly fuckable, but I can't tell Hester that, so I say, "It's police jargon for highly effective."

"Well, I suppose that's encouraging."

"Thank you. Who's Mr. Chambers?"

"My next-door neighbor."

I write it on my pad. "First name?"

"Harrison."

"And what's your issue with him?"

"He killed his wife."

"Really? That's *fantastic!*"

"*Excuse* me?"

"Um...I mean, gosh, that's terrible!"

She gives me a strange look, so I say, "What's her name?"

"Elaine. I mean, it *was* Elaine. Before he murdered her."

"Are you saying he changed his wife's name *after* murdering her?"

She gives me a look. "Are you stupid?"

"Um...some of my questions might not make sense to the untrained ear, but rest assured, there's a purpose for each and every one. In this case, I'm covering all the bases. So tell me, Hester: when did this murder take place?"

"He killed her last week. But I didn't tell the police at first."

"Why not?"

"I wasn't certain. I mean, I knew he'd been *beating* her, but I wasn't positive she was dead. Not at first, anyway."

"What finally convinced you?"

"He moved Elaine's twin sister into his home."

I frown. Hester doesn't *seem* crazy, but then again...

"*This* is what you told the police?"

"Yes."

"And they refused to investigate?"

"Not exactly. They took my statement, then two detectives drove me back to my building, and the three of us went next door to confront Mr. Chambers."

"And how did that go?"

"Harrison told them I was a lunatic."

"Did they search his apartment for Elaine's body?"

"Condo."

"Excuse me?"

"We live in a high-rise condo complex."

"Which one?"

"Lakeshore Towers. And no, they didn't search his condo. Not that it would have mattered."

"Why not?"

"Because he and Elaine's sister removed her body last week."

"How?"

"They rolled her up in a rug and carried her to the elevator."

"You saw this?"

"I saw them carrying a heavy, rolled-up rug to the elevator."

"Was Elaine a small woman?"

"I'd say average. What difference does *that* make?"

"Dead bodies are heavy. I'm not sure they could have carried her very far."

"They placed her in a red wagon. The kind a kid might own."

"So you didn't actually *see* Elaine's body."

"No. But *something* bulky was rolled up in that carpet, and Elaine is no longer in the house."

"The detectives could easily determine if the woman in Harrison's house is Elaine's twin sister."

"You'd think so, but they're saying Elaine never had a twin sister."

"And you think they're lying?"

"I think they're lazy. The woman living with Harrison is the same one who helped him carry the carpet to the elevator. She looks exactly like Elaine, except with blonde hair, not brown, and she didn't have any cuts or bruises on her face."

"Is it possible Elaine changed her hair color and her bruises healed since the last time you saw her?"

"No. Because I saw her that same day, and she had brown hair, a horrendous black eye, and her face was cut and bruised. The corner of her mouth was still caked with blood."

"Where'd you see her?"

"In the elevator."

"I'm surprised she went out in public in that condition."

"Me too. But she was wearing sunglasses, and kept holding her hand in front of her face."

"Did you speak to her?"

"Yes. I asked if she wanted me to go with her to file a police report."

"And she said?"

"She claimed she fell down, and was going to the drug store to get some ointment and bandages."

"But you didn't believe her?"

"Of course not! I heard them arguing the night before, and then..." her voice trails off.

"Then what?"

"Later that night I heard sounds of violence. Like he threw her against the wall. I heard her scream, then cry, then heard a sound like she'd been knocked to the floor. Then everything went quiet, and I never saw or heard another sound from her again."

"Was the twin sister there when you and the detectives showed up?"

"Yes."

"And what did *she* say?"

"She claimed she was Elaine. Said she simply dyed her hair, no big deal."

"And the bruises?"

"She said I made it up. Said she never had any bruises on the elevator, or anywhere else, and the detectives believed her."

"You said the police didn't search Harrison's condo. But did he give them permission to do so?"

"He said they could look around as much as they'd like. But they're lazy as hell. They took one look at Elaine's driver's license, and the rug, and bought his story, hook, line, and sinker."

"What rug?"

"The one they carried to the elevator that night."

"It was *there*? In his *apartment*?"

"Condo."

"Was it the exact same rug? I mean, could he have switched it with a similar one?"

"No. It had the same stain in the same place as the old one."

"Why would he keep the rug he used to dump her body?"

"That's the same thing Harrison and the police asked me. And I told them that was part of the ruse. I said they should take the rug as evidence and run forensic tests on it. But they said it wouldn't help, because the rug had been in their home for years, and they would expect to find Elaine's hair and DNA on it. They said even if they found her blood on the rug it wouldn't be evidence of murder."

"They're right."

She gives me a look. "Does that mean you're on *their* side?"

"No, but it means we're fighting an uphill battle. Was this the first time you heard Harrison and Elaine fighting?"

"No. He'd been hitting her for days."

"Was Elaine a close friend of yours?"

"Why does *that* matter?"

"I'm trying to figure out why you're so concerned about this."

"Are you *serious*? A woman—my next door *neighbor*—has been murdered! Whether or not we got along has nothing to *do* with it! I'm living next door to a *killer*! And now he and Elaine's sister know I'm onto them!"

"Good point."

"My life's in danger!"

"Right. Um...I don't mean to be indelicate, but...I assume you have the means to...ah...*fund* an investigation?"

"How much are we talking about?"

"Five hundred to start."

She frowns. "That sounds like the price a *real* detective would charge."

"Insults have no effect on me. I've stared *death* in the eye."

She appraises me. "I sincerely doubt that."

"Ask around, if you don't believe me."

"I wouldn't know where to start." She thinks a moment, then says, "What does $500 buy me?"

"A preliminary investigation."

"That tells me nothing."

"I'll poke around, check some records, perform surveillance; shake some bushes, see what pops out."

"That sounds awfully nebulous."

I arch a brow.

She says, "You're going to poke *around?* Shake some *bushes?*"

"It's how we private investigators talk. We use a language all our own."

"Why?"

"I don't know. But other professions do it. Doctors and lawyers use Latin, police use codes, politicians use talking points. Certain preachers speak in tongues."

"Maybe so, but your words sounds awfully non-committal."

"It's better than it sounds. Let me put it this way: if there's something going on, I'll find it."

"And *then* what?"

"I'll take the case."

"And what will *that* cost?"

"Five grand."

"G.F.Y., sweetheart."

"What's that mean?"

"Go fuck yourself."

"How about four grand?"

"I'll pay nothing further. I won't *have* to."

"Why not?"

"Because you'd have a legal obligation to take your findings to the police. Otherwise, you'd be guilty of aiding and abetting."

"Actually, there's no duty to report a crime unless a special relationship exists, like between a parent and child." I think a moment, then add, "Except that in some states doctors and teachers are required to report suspected child abuse. Otherwise, no duty to report. Even if you witness a crime taking place."

"I don't believe you."

"Ever heard of Genovese Syndrome?"

"No."

"In 1964 a 28-year-old girl named Kitty Genovese was stabbed to death near her home. A number of neighbors witnessed it, but didn't report. Kitty's name became synonymous with the social psychological phenomenon known as the Bystander Effect."

"That sounds like a bunch of gobbledygook."

"I can cite another case if you like."

"More gobbledygook?"

"In 2009, twenty witnesses watched a 15-year-old California girl get beaten and gang-raped for two hours outside a high school dance. The witnesses laughed, took pictures, and some even participated in the rape. But no one reported the crime, and nor were they charged. What I'm saying, neither you, nor I, have a legal responsibility to report a crime."

Hester gives me a hard look, but doesn't ask for further clarification, which is good, since those are the only cases I've ever memorized. Then I say, "But if I uncover any evidence Harrison murdered his wife, I'll report it."

"Thank you...Asshole!"

"What did you just call me?"

"Asshole. Because it's one thing to charge me $500 to investigate a murder, but you went beyond that and tried to shake me down for another $5,000."

"I said I'd report my findings to the police."

"Yeah. After giving me a lecture about Genovese Syndrome."

"Well—"

Hester opens her purse. "You want the $500 or not?"

I do, and take it quickly, before she changes her mind.

After she leaves I go to Dillon's office and hand him the check, saying, "We're on the case."

"Give me the details," he says.

I do, and finish by expressing my outrage over what she called me.

He laughs. "I'm sorry, Dani, but she's right. You *can* be an asshole sometimes."

"Can *not*!"

"It's okay. I still like you."

"It's *not* okay. People *like* me. *No* one thinks I'm an asshole."

"Whatever."

I put my hands on my hips. "Name one person who thinks that. Even sometimes."

"Me."

"Name another."

"Hester Darrow."

"Name someone I care about."

"Sophie Alexander."

"Someone else."

"Your friend Sarah."

"I have several friends named Sarah."

"I'm referring to the one whose bachelorette party you ruined on Friday. The one who called you an asshole."

"That doesn't count."

He laughs. "How about the lady at the police station who works in sex crimes?"

"Oh yeah? *Ha!*"

"What's that supposed to mean?"

"It means it doesn't count if you don't know her name."

"Christine Herold."

"Christine's a bitch."

"Of course she is. How about...the entire Nashville police department?"

"Wrong! You're forgetting Chris Sutter."

"Sutter *hates* you!"

"Maybe so, but he never called me an asshole."

"So far as you know."

I take a deep breath. Then say, "Dillon? That word is highly offensive to me. I insist you stop using it immediately. Or, at the very least, refer to it as the A-word."

"*A-word?*"

"That's right. You have no idea what that word represents to me. Total strangers have called me that my whole life. People who didn't even *know* me! But it stops today. A new era of political correctness has dawned."

"What are you *talking* about?"

"Times have changed, Dillon, and I expect you and Hester and everyone else to change with them. You're lucky as hell I haven't decided to make you a public example. Because you could lose everything you own if word got out you called me that."

He makes a sweeping gesture with his arm. "Thanks. It'd be a real shame to lose all this."

"Oh yeah? Well maybe I'll wait till you're rich before making it public. I could hold this over your head indefinitely. Piss me off just once and you'll rue the day you called me an A-word. The media will publicly humiliate you and strip you of all your possessions. By the time they're done you'll have to go on *Dancing with the Stars* to repair your image."

"That sounds plausible."

"Don't despair, Dillon. You and I have always been close. We're partners and friends."

"Meaning?"

"If I turn you in someday, I'll give you a chance to publicly repent. Out of the goodness of my heart."

"Thanks. Whatever."

"Don't 'whatever' *me*, Dillon! This is a very serious issue. And anyway, *you're* the asshole."

"Oh, really?"

"That's right...*Asshole!*"

"You like saying that word, don't you?"

"Maybe."

"Which begs the question: if that word is so offensive to you, how come *you're* allowed to say it?"

"I've *earned* the right."

"By doing what?"

I think a moment. "I'm not sure. But I feel very strongly about it."

He sighs. "In that case, I apologize."

"Thank you."

"When do you want to start on Hester's case?"

"Four-thirty."

"Today?"

"Uh huh."

"What's the plan?"

I show him the elevator key Hester gave me before leaving. "Harrison and Elaine's twin sister won't be home till after six."

"We're breaking and entering?"

"Unless you're scared."

"I'm in."

"Good. Now let's talk about that thousand dollar entry I found on last month's P&L."

"Which one?"

"I'd like to think we're making so much money I wouldn't notice a thousand dollar deposit, but since it represented more than half our income, it deserves some scrutiny. The entry says "Doug Ballard.""

"So?"

"Who's that?"

"A guy."

"Thanks for clearing that up. What's his story?"

"He's a friend. I helped him with a project. No big deal."

"If a friend paid you for helping him, why'd you deposit it to our company account?"

"Because I did the work here in the office, on company time."

"What did Doug need?"

Before he can respond, Fanny buzzes Dillon's desk phone: "Sophie's here."

I go to the reception area, but Fanny's alone. "Where's Sofe?"

"In the parking lot."

Don't ask me how Fanny knows this, she just does, and has never been wrong. She claims to hear people getting out of their cars and says she can tell who they are by their gait. Obviously, that's impossible, since we're on the far side of the building, second floor, and our office faces the freeway, not the parking lot. Nor are there any cameras in the parking lot. Nevertheless, within moments the front door opens, and Sofe walks in, notes my expression, and says, "What?"

"Fanny called it."

I wait for Sofe and Fanny to tell each other hi, then lead her back to the conference room where Dillon's putting the final touches on our upcoming presentation.

"You sure it's okay for us to be here?" I ask.

Dillon says, "You should both be here. Mr. Johnson likes the pretty ladies, and it might be the only way to get him to watch the monitor." He looks me over and says, "Can you show a little cleavage?"

I give Soife a "see what I mean?" look, then frown. "That's creepy. The guy's...*how* old?"

"Early 70's." Then adds, "Why? Would it be less creepy if he were 30, and good-looking?"

"Of course."

Dillon says, "Then pretend he's 30."

"What're you, his pimp?"

"Yeah. This is just my day job. By night, I'm Johnny Johnson's pimp. Look, it's just him and his wife. He's got Alzheimer's. He won't remember a thing.

I look at Sofe. "Why can't *she* show a little cleavage for the client?"

Sofe says, "I'd be all wrong for the job."

"Why?"

"He wants you to show a little cleavage, and that's all you've got: a little cleavage."

She laughs.

"Hilarious. Big deal. So I don't have giant globs of fat hanging from my collarbones. You know that's what tits are, right? Globs of fat?"

"Keep telling yourself that," she says, and laughs some more, making me wonder why I invited her in the first place. Then I remember the magical moment we're about to experience.

I sigh, unbutton the second button on my blouse, and wait for the Johnsons to arrive.

Chapter 7

ACCORDING TO LOCAL LORE, Johnny "Sweet Pea" Johnson was the greatest running back who ever played high school football. The only reasons you never heard of him are (1) he played in the 1960's, and (2) all his achievements were removed from the record books following his conviction for murdering a family of six, including two infant children. After serving 44 years in various maximum security prisons, DNA evidence proved him innocent of the crime. By then he had Stage Four Alzheimer's. Over the past two years his condition has grown progressively worse, and is now between stages six and seven. Soon, Johnny will require full-time medical care.

Eight months ago his wife, Sally, hired us to see if we could locate any surviving films of his games. It took scores of Internet posts, phone calls, personal visits, and more than 40 hours of Dillon's expert editing to secure 30 minutes of film highlights, which he converted to video for this special occasion.

Now, with Sweet Pea sitting front and center facing me, I try to direct his eyes to our giant monitor. He's showing zero interest apart from the way he's looking at me, so I signal Dillon to start the video. As he does so, Sally and I exchange a look, knowing Johnny Johnson is about to see himself on film for the first time in his entire life. Sally hopes this will trigger something in his memory to prove his condition hasn't become hopeless.

As the action starts behind me, I get caught up in the moment about how we're all going to be old or dead someday, and when the end of my life approaches I'd hate not remembering my past, or the people I care about, like Sofe, who's sitting there so patiently. A gifted songwriter, Sofe's been working on new tunes all week and would much rather be composing at this moment, but here she sits, showing me total support. I catch her eye and mouth the words, *Thank you.*

She smiles.

When Sweet Pea's rheumy eyes focus on the action, I slide out of his field of vision and watch his reaction from the side. Minutes go by before he suddenly straightens up in his seat and surprises us by shouting, "Damn! Who *is* that?"

Sally says, "It's *you*, Baby. That's you, runnin' the ball."

He says, "This is *bullshit!* Trick photography. No one could *ever* run like that!"

He's right. I mean, you could put everything I know about football into a thimble and have room left over for peas and corn, but even I can see Johnny Johnson crashing through bodies, leaping over players, cutting left and right, changing direction, spinning out of tackles, and sprinting 70, 80, and even 90 yards at a clip.

As he sits there, thoroughly captivated, Sally says, "You know who that is, Baby? That's Sweet Pea Johnson!"

I see a vague sense of recollection enter his eyes, then he moans, and tears start flowing down his cheeks. He lifts his legs to his chest and hugs his knees while rocking back and forth, sobbing like a man who's lost everything, which is exactly how I'd cry if I were him. But I'm crying anyway, just watching this special moment, and that causes Sofe to cry, and pretty soon Sally and Dillon are crying, too. Suddenly Fanny opens the door and shouts, "You'll be happy to know I just got my period! Sadly, I'm going home now." With that, she turns and walks away.

Chapter 8

AFTER 20 MINUTES OF fiddling with Harrison's front door lock, Dillon says, "So much for your claim of master lock-picker."

"It's not as easy as it looks."

"It doesn't look easy at all. How much did you pay for that PI course?"

"The Great Scott Private Eye course is $300, but I haven't bought it yet. I learned all this from the demonstration video they posted on YouTube."

"Maybe you should have paid."

Ten minutes later, Hester exits her condo, walks over and says, "If this is all you've got, I want my money back."

"Sorry, but we're already on the case," I say. "No refunds once we've started."

She shakes her head. "This is the sorriest-ass effort I've ever witnessed. If you think I'm going to pay you $500 to stand in the hall all day wiggling paper clips and bobby pins, you're sadly mistaken."

Dillon says, "I'm not sure what you'll be able to *do* about it."

"Thanks Dillon," I say.

Hester says, "You think you'll have better luck with the key?"

I look up. "What key?"

"The one to Harrison's condo."

"Where is it?"

"In Barbara's condo."

"Where's that?"

She points to the door across the hall and motions us to follow. She unlocks Barbara's door, then removes a key from the top drawer of the desk in Barbara's foyer. Hester hands me the key with this explanation: "We all watch each other's condos when we're out of town. I watch Barbara's, she watches Harrison's, Harrison watches—"

I interrupt. "Who has a key to *your* condo?"

"No one. I never leave town."

"And you didn't think to mention the key situation before leaving my office?"

"I assumed you'd be able to gain entry like those detectives on TV."

"If you had access to Harrison's condo all along, why not search it yourself?"

"I have. Several times. But I'm not sure what to look for. Like you, I'm not a detective."

I frown at her, but gladly use the key to open Harrison's door. Dillon and I enter.

"Did you forget something?" Hester asks.

I give her the key and watch her take it back to Barbara's condo. As she walks down the hall toward the elevator I ask, "Want to join us?"

"I'm going to the grocery store," she says, without bothering to turn around.

I look at Dillon. "We're on our own, pal."

"Not really," a voice says.

Chapter 9

HAD IT BEEN A man's voice, or a threatening one, I would have screamed and peed my pants right there on the cherry wood floor. But it was only scary enough that Dillon and I jumped.

"Relax," the woman says. "Sit down." She presses a button on the remote she's holding, and a muted song starts playing in the background.

Dillon takes a seat, but I know better. If you're sitting in a chair it's harder to defend yourself from an attack. Then again, the only assault taking place is the Steely Dan song.

"You don't seem surprised to see us," I say.

She shrugs. "What can I tell you? We live next door to a crazy person."

I stare at her to memorize her features. "And who are you, exactly?"

"Elaine Chambers. Who else would I be?"

"Elaine's evil twin."

She laughs. "I suppose I owe you an explanation."

"You do?"

"Not really, but I can't have people constantly breaking into my condo, snooping around. What if you'd caught me rubbing one out?"

Dillon's jaw drops.

I, on the other hand, am hip. Worldly. A consummate professional. Nothing fazes me. "What's your dildo of choice?" I ask.

"Is it okay to speak in front of the boy?"

Dillon's face turns red.

"Yes, of course," I say. "He's practically nineteen."

"Well," she says, "Personally, I'm a fan of the *Vibrating Clit Flogger*."

I lied earlier. Everything fazes me. Especially this.

Elaine laughs. "You don't recognize me."

I stare harder.

She says, "I'm Sarah's cousin. I was at the party on Friday."

I work to keep my expression neutral. Then say, "Just so you know, my friend Sofe and I staged that whole thing as a joke."

"Of course you did."

We spend a few minutes talking about Sarah, and it doesn't take long to realize Elaine is exactly who she says is. So I say, "Why does Hester think you killed your sister?"

Elaine smiles. "Hester's the proverbial neighbor from hell. My husband and I have spent months trying to get her to stop obsessing over us."

"What's she done?"

"You name it, she does it. She goes through our trash, steals our mail, sneaks into our house, checks our medicine cabinets, and follows us when we go for walks."

"So you faked your own murder?"

She laughs. "Sort of."

"What about the cuts and bruises Hester saw?"

"You got a few minutes?"

"I guess."

"Follow me."

She leads us to the master bathroom, sits at her makeup desk, reaches into a drawer, and removes several jars of stage makeup. Points to her wide assortment of eye shadows and lipsticks and gives us a running commentary while applying it: "The black eye's simple. All you need is a bit of concealer under the eye and on the lid. Next, I use a small eyeshadow brush to apply a bit of yellow. Then...see this? I use the tip of this reddish-brown lipstick to make random dots around the socket to give the effect of tiny blood vessels. Then I dab a soft purple eyeshadow over the same area, like so. Finally, I use a dark purple eyeshadow right under the eye, and an accent color, like a dark brown matte to form a lower shadow and make the colors pop."

"So it's just *makeup*? Surely Hester could tell."

"Well, I rushed it just now, but even so, can *you* tell it's fake? I mean, if you hadn't watched me do it?"

"I can't," Dillon says.

"The combination of colors gives the impression I attempted to cover the black eye with makeup."

She dabs some more brown around the eye socket. "For the finish, I use a plum colored blush, like so."

It suddenly comes together for me. "I have to admit, it's pretty convincing."

"Not only that, but in the hallway and elevator, with sunglasses on..."

"It's diabolical!"

"Thank you."

"What about the swelling?"

"The lumps require bunion pads, resins, and more eye shadow. I'd show you, but those take about 20 minutes. But here's how I make the cuts and dried blood..."

She walks us through the process, and I'm astonished with the results.

"How did you learn all this?"

"My friend's a part-time makeup artist. She does Little Theater and stage productions. As you can see, it's not hard. I could teach you everything I know in the space of an hour."

Dillon laughs. "It just dawned on me."

"What's that?"

"Dani was in the hallway, working on your door for half an hour, and you were sitting here the whole time, waiting for her."

"I'm usually better," I say, scowling at Dillon. Then add, "So why didn't you let us in sooner?"

Elaine smiles. "It took me all that time to locate a Steely Dan song to commemorate the occasion of your break in."

I listen a minute. "*Turn That Heartbeat Over Again?*"

Dillon says, "It's a song about a robbery gone bad."

Elaine says, "That part's a coincidence. I just wanted anything by Steely Dan. I thought you might pick up on the hint."

"Which hint is that?"

"Are you not familiar how the band got its name?"

I shrug. "I guess I assumed some guy named Dan was the singer, and he had steely blue eyes, or something."

She laughs. "Not even close. The band stole the name from *Naked Lunch*, by William S. Burroughs. In the novel, Steely Dan was a steam-powered dildo."

"Omigod! You swear?"

"Yup."

"Who would have thought?"

"Everyone who read the novel."

"Do people still read novels?"

"Just cool people."

"Is it like a secret society or something?"

"Yes. But I can get you in."

"What would I have to do?"

"Read certain books."

"That's it?"

She nods. "Do that and you'll be One of Us in no time."

I frown. "Is this a sneaky way to make me read the classics?"

"The books I'm talking about are anti-classics. They're the opposite of literature."

I'm confused, and my expression proves it. "What's the opposite of literature?"

"Fun!"

"I love fun! When can I start?"

"Next chapter."

Chapter 10

"SHALL I EXPLAIN THE whole caper?" Elaine says.

"Please."

She tells us how she talked Harrison into faking a couple of fights. "These weren't long, drawn-out affairs," she says. "Nothing that would cause other neighbors to call the police. But afterward, I'd put on the makeup and make sure Hester saw me. After a couple of weeks of this, I did something I always wanted to do."

"Change your hair color?"

"Exactly. Then we staged the whole body-in-the rug thing, so Hester would freak out."

"She called the cops, you removed the makeup, and made her look like a fool."

"Yes. But there was more to the ruse."

"What do you mean?"

"We had to sneak the rug back in without her seeing us. That was tricky, because she was watching the hallway the whole time. We couldn't do it till she went to the police station. But there's more: even though she saw us carrying the rug down the hallway that night, Hester wasn't sure I was dead. So I went about my business as a blonde, and a few days later she called, and I answered the phone, disguising my voice enough so she'd think I was someone else. She asked if she could come over, and I said yes, and she quizzed me about things only I would know. Meaning, Elaine. Of course, I purposely screwed up the interview, and that convinced her to go to the police. When the detectives showed up, she asked me a whole new set of questions only Elaine would know, and I aced them."

"Then she hired us."

"Yes. And here we are."

I look at Dillon. "You believe her?"

He nods.

"I do too."

She says, "I know Hester had it coming, but now I feel sort of bad. We should probably confess."

I say, "Can you do me a favor?"

"Name it."

"Can we bring Hester here and make it look like we caught you playing a practical joke on her? That will help make up for how badly I botched the lock-picking."

She thinks it over. "I guess so. You want to bring her when she gets back from the grocery, or wait till Harrison gets home around nine?"

"Can we put it off till next week?"

"Why?"

"I want to make sure her check clears."

Chapter 11

IT'S HAPPY HOUR, and Sofe's stuck in traffic, so I grab us two chairs at the counter of the trendy rooftop bar in downtown Nashville and tell the bartender, "One beer, please."

He stares at me, so I say, "I only need one beer, not two."

His blank expression, causes me to add: "It's happy hour. Two for one, right? My girlfriend's about to join me, but she doesn't approve of beer. She thinks it's gauche. No offense. So anyway, I just want to order one, and don't need the free one. And just so you know, I only plan to take a couple of sips. Then I'm going to push it away and pretend it was someone else's."

He says, "Thanks for the epic. But all I care about is what type of beer do you want?"

"Whatever type main characters get."

"I have no idea what that means."

"In the movies, the main character bellies up to the bar, asks for a beer, and the bartender always knows which one she wants."

He shakes his head. "Never heard that before, and I've heard a lot. Fine, I'll pick one. But if you don't like it, you can't have your money back."

"Why not?"

"Because this is a bar, not an ice cream store. We don't give free samples." He eyes me carefully and says, "You understand this?"

I nod. Then say, "Movies are so much better than real life."

"Tell me about it. Just once I'd like to slide a filled beer mug the whole length of the bar."

"Why don't you?"

"It'll either hit the edge, fall and crash on the floor, or hit a wet or dry spot and spill all over the counter, not to mention whatever customer happens to be nearby."

"Yeah, but don't you get lots of hot, sexy women at closing time?"

He laughs. "Are *you* planning to still be here at closing time?"

"When's that?"

"My point exactly. Hot, sexy women have better places to be."

"Sofe and I stay out pretty late."

"That's your girlfriend?"

I nod.

"What's late to you guys?"

"Midnight."

He laughs. "Closing time's four."

"In the *morning*?"

"Yup."

"What does that do to your *skin*?"

"Four a.m. ladies don't worry about such things as skin tone."

The beer tasted thick and syrupy, but satisfying. Nevertheless, I pushed it away when Sofe came through the front door. Now she and I are nursing our second drink, and I've told her all about Hester and Elaine, and how Elaine is Sarah's cousin, and how she faked her own death to teach Hester a lesson.

"Is she cute?"

"*Hester*? God no!"

"I'm referring to Sarah's cousin. Elaine."

I shrug. "She's okay."

"Okay means hot."

"In this case it means slightly above average. A seven, at most."

"*I'm* a seven."

"You're a nine and you know it!"

She looks down and smiles. Then asks, "Did she turn you on?"

"Not in the least." I pause. "You believe me?"

"Strangely, yes." She sighs. "I wish *something* would turn you on. Something besides what's-her-face."

"What's-her-face? Who's *that*?" I roll my eyes. "Wait. You're not talking about—"

"Bethy? Who else? Surely you remember Bethy: teacher of the year? The one you cheated on me with? The one you—"

"I remember!" I say, holding both hands up in protest before she has a chance to enumerate the sexual acts Beth and I performed. Because once *that* shit enters the conversation, it's over. I never should have told her what happened in Beth's bedroom. Then again, it was the main component of Sophie's Terms of Forgiveness: in order to put this behind us once and for all she required my complete honesty and full disclosure.

So I spilled my guts.

Reluctantly.

Afterward, every minute, sordid detail of the affair was revealed, parsed, discussed, hashed and rehashed till I thought my head would explode. And each activity she forced me to reveal, including the feelings I experienced while doing them, took Sofe through the five stages of grief.

It was a lengthy, agonizing process for both of us, and I stupidly believed...

"I thought we were past that," I say.

"I won't apologize for bringing it up."

"You never do. Shall I say it again? I'm sorry, Sofe. I was confused. It was a rotten thing to do." I look into her eyes to see if I've said enough.

I haven't.

So I add, "I hit rock bottom. Stabbed you in the back. Debased myself. Abandoned you. Spit on our relationship. Treated you like pond scum. Lost your trust."

"You're sugar-coating again."

Seriously?

I fight the urge to scream *Go fuck yourself!* Because groveling for forgiveness for something she's already forgiven is part of the ongoing, never-ending process of living with a woman. It is so much freaking *work!*

So I say, "You're right, of course. I was beastly, but your love brought me to my senses. The day you took me back was the luckiest day of my life."

"And?" she says.

"And I would never do anything to ruin what we have." I put my hand on hers, and show her my sweetest, most tender look. Not because I'm feeling the love right now, but because I just spent a weekend in Sophie's doghouse, and have no desire to come home to a fucking war zone for the next six weeks. And that's exactly what will happen if I fail to diffuse the Beth discussion immediately.

This is something you learn quickly when dating and living with a woman: if you cheat on her and she takes you back she'll never put it completely behind her. Half the things you say or do—no matter how innocent—will trigger something in her memory to tie to your former indiscretion. When I returned to Sofe after concluding my brief affair, I may as well have brought Beth home to live with us, because Sofe sees her everywhere, in everything I say and do. If I buy a new pair of panties, it's, "Oh, how nice! Is that what Bethy wears?" If I change my brand of toothpaste or shampoo, it's: "Should I worry? Are you cheating again?" If I kiss her in a slightly different way, or use an expression she hasn't heard before, it's "Did you get that from Bethy?"

And I'll tell you something else: her name's Beth Conroy, not Bethy. To the best of my knowledge, no one in the world has ever called her Bethy. Sofe calls her that to piss me off.

And it does.

Not sure why I give a shit what she calls Beth, but the word *Bethy*—or the derogatory way she says it—annoys the crap out of me. Not to mention the way she dogs Beth, as in: "I don't understand what you saw in her. I mean, if she were the *least* bit attractive..." Of course these types of comments are minefields, always uttered while studying my facial expression to see how I react. Because one thing we both know is Beth Conroy is super hot. But I dare not defend her, ever. So I say, "I thought we put all this behind us."

"We did," she says. "And I forgave it. But I can't forget it."

"Right. Um...tell me again why that is?"

"Because that event was a septic overflow in our relationship. Fucking Beth Conroy was like putting a dead body in my car for two weeks: I'll never get rid of the stench. And the only good that came from it is the painful reminder of what happens when you think with your twat instead of your brain. The grass is *not* greener in Bethy's yard. Or anyone else's."

I decide this isn't the time to point out she's mixing metaphors and idioms. So I say, "Absolutely right. But the good news is I learned my lesson. You can trust me. I'll never do it again."

"Never do what, Dani? Fuck Bethy? Or never look at another woman?"

"Both."

"I hear you saying that, but then again, we're not exactly having *sex*, are we!"

I look around the bar. "Think you can say that a little louder?"

"Sorry. I know how you hate for people to think we're having a romantic relationship."

I sigh, keep my mouth shut. Mercifully, she does the same. Then, early into our third drink, she says, "You know what I miss?"

"Tell me."

"Sexual role-playing. Remember how that always loosened you up?"

I smile. "Fun times. Remind me again why we had to stop?"

"You said it was politically incorrect."

"I did?"

"When those teachers got caught having sex with their students you said the whole teacher/schoolgirl construct turned creepy for you."

"Maybe we could come up with a different scenario."

"Really?" she says. "Like what?"

"I don't know."

She says, "How about lesbian boss seduces her new employee?"

"Sexual harassment in the workplace? *Seriously* Sofe?"

"It would be *consensual!*"

"*All* role-playing's consensual. But it wouldn't be politically correct."

She sighs. "Why does sex have to be politically correct for everyone except politicians?"

"I don't know. It just does."

Undeterred, she says, "What if we dress up like other people and pretend to meet in a bar?"

"Then we may as well be *dating* other people."

"What if one of us pretends to be asleep and the other one—" Seeing my arched eyebrow she says, "Uh, never mind."

She whips out her phone.

"What now?"

"I'm gonna look up the top ten role-playing games for lesbians."

"*Lesbians?*"

"Sorry. I meant to say...uh...wait. What are you calling yourself these days?"

"Sexually curious."

"Right. Well, what I meant to say is in the event there are no role-playing fantasies for sexually-curious ladies, I thought we might want to check out the top 10 lesbian fantasies. You know, just to see what *those* girls are up to."

"Good idea."

After a quick search Sofe informs me there are zero fantasies listed for sexually curious young ladies, but hundreds for gay girls.

"Read some," I say. "But not too loudly."

"First is...well, that's funny."

"What?"

"Teacher seduces schoolgirl."

I frown. "What's the second?"

"Schoolgirl seduces teacher."

I arch a brow. "Underage sex in return for good grades? Wrong on so many levels!"

She says, "Third one sounds interesting: Lady of the manor seduces maid."

"Coercion. Sexual subjugation."

"What are you, a lawyer?" She sighs. "What if we flipped it?"

"To what?"

"Maid seduces lady of the manor."

"Prostitution?"

She frowns. "That's a stretch."

"What else have you got?"

"Conquering queen ravages vanquished foe?"

"That's rape, Sofe."

"Mad scientist builds creature for sex?"

"Would this be a living, breathing creature?"

"I would think so."

"Then it's sex without consent."

"Okay. Next is...uh, never mind."

"What?"

"Even *I* can see the problem," she says.

"Tell me anyway."

"Nurse seduces mental patient."

"*Eew!*"

Sofe says, "Here's one. Deprogrammer seduces cult follower." When I don't respond right away she says, "Pretty inventive, don't you think?"

"Best yet," I say, "but the cult follower would be vulnerable. She wouldn't be in a position to make an informed decision."

"You're aware these are fantasies, right?"

"Of course. Read on."

She pauses a minute, then says, "I'm skipping the next three."

"Why?"

"Too close to home."

"Let me guess: kidnapper/victim?"

"Yup. And similar themes."

"What's after those?"

"Nun seduces novice."

"Sacrilegious."

She reads a moment, then grins. "Police woman performs cavity search for contraband."

"No thanks."

"You sure?" she says, spreading imaginary butt cheeks in the air with her hands.

"Is that supposed to represent my ass?" I say.

She grins.

I frown. "You are such a guy sometimes."

She scrolls a while, reading silently. Then says, "*Jackpot!*"

"What?"

"Even *you* can't complain about this one!"

"*Excuse* me? You make it sound like I'm being difficult."

"*You?* Never!"

"What's the fantasy?"

"This is just too good."

"Tell me."

"Sexually curious girl asks lesbian best friend to introduce her to gay sex."

My eyes go wide. "*Seriously?*"

She nods. "There's more. It says, "The sexually curious girl wants to experience every aspect of lesbian lovemaking. Every aspect, Dani!"

"*Asshole!*"

"Yes, that would certainly be an aspect."

"*What? No!* I mean, *you're* an asshole!"

"Why?"

"You made that one up."

She winks.

I say, "And anyway, the lesbian seducing the curious girl is just normal sex for us."

"Except for the part where I get to do everything to you."

"Don't be gross."

She sighs.

After five minutes of quiet, I ask, "Are you pouting?"

"Why shouldn't I?"

"Because I've come up with the perfect fantasy."

"Don't fuck with me."

"I'm not. It's great. Better than anything on the list. And there's nothing politically incorrect about it."

"Bullshit!"

"I'm serious."

"Really?"

I nod.

"Okay then, tell me."

"I'm still inventing it."

"What have you got so far?"

"The name: *Countdown*."

She cocks her head. "Sounds interesting. What's the concept?"

"I'll tell you later."

"When?"

"Just before we do it."

"When will *that* be?"

"Soon."

"You swear?"

"Yeah. I mean, I have to sleep on it."

"Why?"

"It's a terrifying concept, and naughty as hell."

"Gotta say, I'm intrigued!"

"Good. Can we get some dessert now?"

"We're skipping dinner?"

"Dessert rules."

"Agreed. What are you craving?"

"An Absurdity Sundae. But that's not gonna happen."

"Why not?"

"Because it's an ice cream dish that costs sixty grand."

"Shut *up!*"

"I'm serious."

"Then someone's grievously overcharging."

"It's not just ice cream, it's a travel experience, too. They fly you first class to Tanzania, put you up in a five-star hotel, and the next day a climbing expert guides you to the top of Mount Kilimanjaro, where they create your desert from fresh glacial ice."

"You have to climb a mountain to get your dessert?"

"Think of it as an adventure."

"I'll try, but it still sounds overpriced. And chilly."

"The founder of the ice cream company says he'll personally hand-churn a batch of ice cream using the glacial ice found at the summit."

"So?"

"I think it's a nice touch. Plus, you get a t-shirt."

"Yippee. Sorry, but the whole thing sounds wasteful. And you know what else? That's exactly the sort of thing that makes foreigners hate Americans."

"Anyone can buy the sundae, not just Americans."

"Still, with all the poor people in the world, it's a ridiculous extravagance, and—"

"The balance of the money goes to an African charity to protect the environment."

She purses her lips. "You're making that up."

"Nope. They promise to donate five figures to a non-profit."

"Well, in that case...count me in."

"I would, except...if we *both* go it'll cost $85,000."

"Would I get a t-shirt?"

"If not, you can have mine."

"You're so generous, offering to give me a t-shirt you could never possibly hope to get."

"I know, right? You're welcome."

She's suddenly staring bug-eyed.

"What's wrong?"

"We *know* him!"

"Who?"

She points to the TV above the bar. "We *know* him!"

I look at the picture on the screen. "He looks sort of familiar, but…"

Then they flash his name: *Tommy Kern.* Followed by: *Stabbed to death.*

"Holy *shit!*"

"We know him, right?"

I nod. "I don't believe it!"

"What?"

"She fucking killed him."

"Who?"

"Abbey Rayne."

Chapter 12

"REFRESH ME," SOFE SAYS.

"I can't. You know how I hate backstory."

"Short version."

"Abbey Rayne's the college sophomore that got raped six months ago."

"Right! And you investigated this guy..."

"Tommy Kern."

"And he was guilty, right?"

"Totally. Dillon hacked the school records and found he had six prior rape accusations. But the school did nothing."

"This was what, six months ago?"

"About that."

"And Abbey went after him, right?"

"She did. But they never brought the case to court. Said there wasn't enough evidence to convict."

"So they expelled him?"

"No. His total punishment was to write a one-page essay on date rape."

"That's insane!"

"I agree. And so does Abbey."

"And you think she killed him?"

"I know she did."

"How?"

I lower my voice. "She asked me to find her a hitman."

Sofe's eyes grow large. "You never told me that!"

"It never amounted to anything because I claimed I didn't have those types of connections, and reminded her that on TV they always turn out to be undercover cops."

"In other words, you lied."

"Yup."

"You could have called Uncle Sal, or put her in touch with Donovan Creed, or Callie Carpenter, but chose not to. Why?"

"I thought it was a slippery slope, her being an angry college student and all. What if she told a friend? You know how girls talk. Eventually they'd have a fight, and if her friend tells the wrong person, I'll be on the six o'clock news with the cops leading me out of my office in nickel-plated handcuffs."

"How do you know she didn't hire someone on her own?"

I point to the screen. "Twenty-seven stab wounds? No way. This was personal."

"What are you gonna do?"

"I can't believe I'm saying this, but I think I have to call the police."

"You'd turn her *in?*"

"No. I mean, I'm sure she's on their radar, 'cause who'd have a better motive? She tried to take Tommy to court; failed, then got suspended for claiming the college was engaged in a cover up."

"Which they were."

"Of course they were. But what could *she* do about it? In order to get reinstated, she had to publicly apologize. Then, when all the publicity died down, they rescinded her scholarship."

"So her punishment for getting raped was worse than his punishment for raping her."

"Sucks, right?"

"And now she's killed him. You want my opinion?" She takes a sip from her cocktail glass. "The bastard had it coming."

"I agree. But I'd hate to see her go to prison for it. Especially if it's my testimony that seals her fate."

"Here's a novel idea: don't tell the cops. She's your client, after all."

"*Was* my client. And I really liked her, and felt awful for her. But this is too important to withhold. They need to know, and I need to tell them."

"Dani? Please don't."

"It's not like I *want* to."

She thinks a minute. "Is there any doubt he raped her?"

"None. And six others, as well."

"Then he deserved it. And you know what else? She deserves to get away with it."

"Maybe so. But that's not how the law works."

She stares into my eyes. "If it had been me instead of Abbey Rayne, would you tell the cops?"

"Of course not!"

"Why?"

"I love you."

"How does that change things?"

"I don't know. It just does."

We're quiet till Sofe says, "Do you think she'll kill herself?"

"No. Even at her angriest, Abbey was amazingly stable."

"Is she a danger to others?"

"I wouldn't *think* so. I mean, she's only nineteen. Then again…"

"What?"

"Billy the Kid was only eighteen when he killed his first victim."

She gives me a look. "Billy the Kid? How many drinks have you had?"

"Three, same as you."

"On empty stomachs."

"Right."

"Don't call the cops. Wait a few days and see what happens."

"Okay."

I remove my phone from my handbag, search for a number, then call it.

Sofe says, "What are you doing?"

"Calling the police."

"I thought we just agreed to—"

"Relax. They're not gonna take my call. I'll leave a message saying I have some information that could help their case. They'll ignore it, but at least I can prove later on that I tried to contact them the moment I heard the news."

After leaving the message, I look up another number.

"*Now* what are you doing?"

"Calling Abbey."

Sofe frowns. "You have a college girl's phone number in your contact list?"

"She's a former client. I save all my former clients' numbers."

"Why?"

"They each have unique backgrounds, skill sets, and contacts. You'd be surprised how many times they've given me a helping hand with problems I couldn't solve on my own."

"*That's* your story?"

"It is. Plus, keeping their names on file helps me screen my calls. When my phone rings and a name pops up, I know if it's a former client. Why are you asking about this?"

"Because it sounds awfully sexual to me."

I shake my head. *This* again? *For the love of God!* I try to keep the annoyance out of my voice as I ask, "*Sexual?* What are you *talking* about?"

"Abbey's unique *skill* set? And how she gives you a *helping hand* with problems you can't solve on your *own?*"

"Sofe?"

"Yeah?"

"Don't do that."

I press Abbey's number. When she answers I ask, "Where are you?"

"In a bar with friends. Celebrating!"

"That was awfully quick, considering the news just came out on TV."

"Yeah, we saw it too just now. But that's the *official* announcement. We're on campus, remember? We've known about it for over an hour."

"Have the police contacted you?"

"Nope, but I'm gonna call them after my next drink."

"Not a good idea."

"Why not? *I* didn't kill the bastard."

"If they don't already know who did it, they'll probably make you the prime suspect."

"Not gonna happen. I have the perfect alibi."

"That's a red flag right there. Most innocent people don't have proper alibis."

She laughs. "Maybe I'm drunk already, because what you just said sounds absurd. If I have a perfect alibi, I couldn't have done it."

"Maybe they'll think you hired someone to kill him."

She pauses. Then asks, "Why would they think that?"

Chapter 13

"BECAUSE IF THE POLICE ASK, I'll have to tell them about the hitman."

That throws Abbey for a loop: "I thought our conversations were private, or whatever it's called."

"Privileged?"

"Yeah. Aren't they?"

"You're thinking of attorney-client privilege."

"So you'd tell the cops I said that?"

"If they asked? Yes. I'd have to."

"Why would they come to you in the first place?"

"You hired us to investigate Tommy, and we uncovered the six other rape accusations against him, and interviewed his accusers. That discovery became a matter of public record when you tried to take him to court."

She thinks a minute. "Well, it's not an issue. I didn't do it, and didn't hire anyone, so there's nothing to worry about."

"Glad to hear it. But please don't contact the police. Wait till they contact you. And when they do, don't speak to them without an attorney. I can't emphasize this strongly enough."

"Why?"

"Because as you well know, the system sucks. It does *not* work in your favor. If the police want to talk to you, it's because you're already a suspect. Talking to them will *never* help you, but like they say on TV, *everything* you say can be used against you, even if you're innocent. Even your *demeanor* can be used against you. Don't *ever* talk to the police, Abbey. Not ever!"

She laughs. "Even to confess?"

"Especially then. Because an attorney might be able to get you a deal. But if you confess, you'll give the police an airtight case, and the courts will give you a harsher penalty."

"Okay. Whatever."

"Please say it."

"I won't talk to the police without an attorney." She adds, "I promise."

"Thank you. Can I tell you one last thing while we're on the subject?"

She sighs. "Go ahead. But you're killing my celebration buzz."

"Try to remember the cops have no authority to make you a deal, or grant leniency. They'll make you *think* they do, but it's not true. Always remember they don't like you, don't want to help you, and don't care what happens to you. If they're able to browbeat you into making a statement they can use to make a *case* against you, you're screwed. Even if you're innocent, and even if *they* think you're innocent."

"Got it. Thanks."

"Abbey?"

"Yeah?"

"Will you keep me in the loop if anything happens?"

"If I do, are you gonna charge me?"

"No."

"Then, okay."

"Good. Because if things go badly, I might be able to help."

"I'll keep that in mind."

The moment I hang up, Sofe starts in on me: "You just made me feel like Heinz Ketchup."

"What are you talking about?"

"Like I've been with the wrong mustard all these years."

"Come again?"

"I feel like I don't know you."

I take a deep breath, but decide against responding.

She says, "You told Abbey you want to help her, yet you're going to tell the police about the hitman. That's duplicitous."

"I disagree. It's my duty as a citizen to tell the police about the hitman. And it's my duty as a friend to help Abbey if she needs me."

"She won't *need* your help if you don't rat her out to the cops, Dani. And anyway, didn't you just lecture her about never offering information to the police?"

"That's for suspects and potential suspects."

"How would you feel if your comments put her behind bars for 20 years?"

"Horrible."

"Maybe you should think about that before going to the cops."

"Maybe I will."

"Fine."

"Fine!"

Chapter 14

THE WEEKEND FIGHT, followed by tonight's conversation about Beth Conroy, plus the four cocktails we ultimately drank, obligates me to spend the night in Sophie's bed, which is something I rarely do, as it always ends with raw nipples, and swollen other stuff, and...

The next morning I wake up screaming.

Sofe, startled, shouts, "What's happened?"

"Omigod!" I shout. "*Omigod!*"

"What's wrong?"

I stand up in the middle of the bed. "Be honest with me!"

"Of course! What's wrong?"

"Promise you'll tell the truth?"

"You're scaring me. Are you in pain?"

"Worse!"

"What's wrong?"

I make a slow turn. "Do I look like I gained weight?"

"Since when?"

"Last night."

She sighs.

"I'm *serious*, Sofe."

"Then...yeah. You better be careful. Another ten pounds you might wind up a size 2."

"I *knew* it! All night I dreamt about that damn Absurdity Sundae! Wherever I went in my dream, the sundae followed. Finally I tasted it, just to make it go away, you know?"

She shakes her head. "No, I don't."

"But it tasted so incredible I couldn't stop eating it. And that's when I realized I was a helpless pawn in the toils of Beelzebub."

"Excuse me?"

"It's an expression."

"So is this: you're insane."

"I gained a pound in my sleep."

"You woke up screaming for *this*?"

"They're coming. You've got to hide me."

"Who are we talking about?"

"The fat police. Don't let them get me."

Sofe lets out a yawn. "Most people have alarm clocks. Not me. Know why?"

"You've got me?"

"That's right. I live in Dani Land."

"Some friend *you've* turned out to be. Making jokes while I'm in crisis mode."

Sofe interlocks her fingers, stretches her arms high over her head. "Do I really need to point out you can't gain weight while sleeping?"

"Oh yeah? Well tell that to your pregnant cousin!"

"There's a very mundane explanation for what happened to Alice. It's called sleep sex. She drank too much, fell asleep, her husband banged her...cue the baby."

I step off the bed, approach the full-length mirror, aim my butt at it, look over my shoulder.

Sofe says, "Remember the time you woke up screaming after dreaming you were falling off a cliff?"

"What about it?"

"You didn't fall."

"Not *yet*, you mean."

"And that time you woke up screaming because you dreamt you were driving downhill on a winding road and your brakes went out?"

"So?"

"You didn't die in a car crash, did you?"

"It could happen today."

"Go check the bathroom scale. I bet you lost a pound."

I glance at the bathroom door. "I'm scared."

"You can do this, Dani."

"Come with me. *Please?*"

"No problem. I have to pee anyway."

"Fine. But I'm peeing first. It'll help bring my weight down."

"You'll weigh even less if you strip naked."

"I plan to. But you can't look."

"Why?"

"Because I love you, Sofe, and I can't allow you to see me with fat globules oozing from every pore of my body. I probably look like a giant butter sculpture melting in the sun."

"Shut up and get on the scale."

I pee, then climb on the scale to find Sofe was right: I lost a pound.

When I step down, she tries it and says, "Son of a bitch!"

"What's wrong?"

She grits her teeth. "I gained a pound."

"You'll be fine," I say.

"That's *it*? That's all the reassurance you've got for me? I'll be *fine*? We ate and drank the exact same amount yesterday! How could I possibly gain the same amount you lost?"

"It's just a *pound*, Sofe. Let's not make such a big deal out of it, okay? Now, if you'll excuse me, I need to remain here, in front of the mirror a while."

"Why?"

"I have to practice my facial expressions."

She watches as I form my lips into a small circle and say "Oooh!" with wide eyes, then "*Whaat?*" as I work to get the maximum surprise into my expression without creating wrinkles between my brows.

"You've gotta be kidding me," she says.

"What?"

"This is crazy."

"Too severe?" I say.

"No. You. This is...too crazy to watch." She walks away muttering, "It must be tough being gorgeous."

"Don't pout, Sofe. We'll get that pound off you in no time."

Now, at the office, I ask Dillon to print out everything he can find about the Tommy Kern murder. As he types, I notice something: "What's wrong with your computer?"

"Nothing."

"I think it's broken."

"Trust me, it's working fine." He glances at me. "Why do you ask?"

"On TV, when the geek types on a computer, every keystroke clicks or clacks."

He says, "Your knowledge of computers is alarmingly primitive."

"How so?"

"First, no one types on a computer. They type on a keyboard. Second, keyboards are virtually silent. Otherwise, they'd be extremely annoying."

"Not on TV. And you know why?"

"I'm breathless to hear."

"Because it only takes seconds for the brilliant computer genius guy to hack into NASA, or the Pentagon, or whatever. Meanwhile, it's taking *you* five minutes to locate a local news story. You know what I think?"

"I *never* know."

"I think the reason they're faster than you is because their computer keys click and clack."

"That *must* be it."

"You should order a new one tomorrow."

"Really? I can get a new computer?"

"Keyboard. And make sure you get a really loud one."

He hands me the stories and I take them to my office to read while sitting in my outrageously expensive chair. Sure enough, the police named Abbey Rayne a person of interest and have detained her for interrogation. After reading the comments, I buzz Dillon. He enters my office and says, "You think she did it?"

"At first, yes. Absolutely. But then I realized she was the first person questioned."

"So?"

"In the movies, the first person questioned is never the one who's guilty. But you know what's refreshing about this particular crime scene? In a weird way?"

"What's that?"

"No one said what they always say on TV: that this is the most gruesome crime they've ever seen in their 20 years on the police force."

He says, "You're right. I was watching *Dateline* last night, and the detectives were talking about a cold case and said it was the worst crime scene they ever witnessed. Said they still have nightmares about it."

"I bet they say that in every episode. Meanwhile, this kid got stabbed 27 times, and no one's saying that. You know why?"

"Because our local cops have seen worse?"

"Exactly. And isn't *that* a scary thought?"

We're quiet till he says, "Ever notice in the movies how no one ever finishes their meals?"

"What do you mean?"

"When two people meet in a restaurant, they order food, talk a few minutes, then one of them gets up and leaves before the food arrives."

"I do that."

"You do?"

"Sometimes. But you know what bothers *me*?"

"Everything."

"True. But also, why is it that in every movie or TV show that involves the Bible, everyone talks in a British accent?"

"*What?*"

"Even the *Romans* talk in British accents!"

While he thinks about it, I say, "Romans are Italians, right? Just once I'd like to see a movie about the Bible where the Romans say: 'Hey, Mama, Mary: how abouta you bringa you kid over to our house a' for soma veal parm?'" ~"And she'll say, 'No cana do! He lika spaghetti!'"

Dillon stares at me.

"What?"

"Two things: first, that was terribly racist. And second, it makes no sense."

"Why?"

"You just gave an example of a conversation where Romans were speaking broken English."

"So?"

"Your whole point was you wanted the language to be authentic. If it was authentic they should've been speaking Italian."

"I don't *understand* Italian."

"You don't understand a lot of things."

"Oh yeah? Well, I understand that when women on TV turn off the lights to go to bed the room should be darker, but it's not. And the next morning these same women wake up in full makeup, with perfect hair. Ever notice *that*?"

"No. Then again, I've never woken up in bed with a woman, so I'm afraid you'll have to explain why that's a myth."

"It's common sense, Dillon. You can't go to bed wearing makeup, because it'll rub off on your bedding. I learned this the hard way, when I passed out looking great and the next morning my pillow looked like someone used it to suffocate a clown."

"I love it when someone on TV hits the hero on the head with a gun and knocks him out, but he comes to right after the guy leaves. He shakes his head once or twice, makes a joke, tells everyone it's nothing, and within seconds he's back on the case." He laughs. "Unlike you."

"Shut up, Dillon!"

He's right, though. In real life if someone smacked your head with a gun you'd probably die. It hasn't happened to me, thank God, but Dillon's referring to the time someone smacked my head with a slapjack. And even though that's just a flat piece of hard leather with a small weight on the end, I screamed like hell and threw up and pissed my pants and cried my eyes out and went to the hospital and had to stay there overnight. Next day I felt so sorry for myself I said, "Screw the case!" and spent the next three days in bed with puffy eyes, feeling sorry for myself. I pouted and took pain pills and complained to everyone who'd listen how bad my head hurt and how much I hated my life. I was the world's biggest bitch. After a week I finally went back to work, but for the next month I had night sweats, headaches, and double vision. Now, if someone even *acts* like they're gonna hit me over the head I'll surrender all my possessions before being asked.

He says, "Are we gonna stage another break in?"

"Where?"

"Abbey Rayne's apartment."

"She lives in a sorority house."

"Whoa. *That* won't be easy!"

"Why would we do it even if we could?"

"To gather evidence."

"About what?"

He laughs. "You had me gather all this data about her, so I assume you want to investigate her guilt or innocence."

"I ask you to pull up lots of stuff on your computer."

"True. But this time you've got that look in your eye."

"What look?"

"The one that says we're about to take on another free case."

"You think you know me so well."

"Just the part about how we always seem to work for free."

"Stop complaining. It's character building."

"How much character can two people possibly need?"

Chapter 15

I DID WHAT SOPHIE ASKED: I thought it through before talking to the police.

In fact, I waited a full two days after Abbey had been named a person of interest in the investigation. But this morning the police publicly announced she was no longer a suspect. They said she came forward on her own, had cooperated fully, and her alibi checked out. I don't want to get her in trouble, but I can't let her get away with murder either. If she hired a hitman, the police need to know.

So here I am, in the police station, walking down the corridor toward the desk sergeant, who seems in a good mood till he looks up and recognizes me. As I mentioned earlier, the police aren't particularly fond of me. Why? Two reasons: one, I solved a high profile crime they couldn't, and two, I'm always perky. Somehow, that annoys them. If you were to ask anyone in the station why they don't like me, I bet almost all would say it's because I'm too perky. Too bubbly. I'm always "up."

Want me to prove it? No problem, we can start with Frank, the Desk Sergeant.

"Hi, Frank!" I say cheerfully.

"What now?" he says, with great irritation.

Time to test my theory: "You don't seem happy to see me."

"What gave you the first clue?"

"Your attitude. If I didn't know better I'd swear you don't like me."

"I don't."

"Why not?"

"How many reasons do you need?"

"Just one."

"Your high heels."

"Excuse me?"

"You wear high-fashion clothes into the police station. Your heels clip and clop and reverberate through the walls and halls. We can hear you 200 feet away, and it's annoying as hell."

"That's it? That's the reason you hate me?"

"No. But you said to name just one thing. Why are you here?"

"I need to speak to Lieutenant Palmer."

"Why?"

"I have some information about the Tommy Kern murder."

"Have a seat. I'll buzz him."

A moment later he motions me to approach. I do, and he says, "You can see him now. Need an escort?"

"No, but thank you."

"I wasn't offering you one."

"Frank?"

"Yeah?"

"I'd like us to be friends."

"Why?"

"Because we see each other from time to time, and it would be nice if we were friendly, that's all."

He thinks it over. "You mean like we'd have each other's back? That sort of thing?"

I smile. "Exactly. What if I stopped wearing high heels when I come to the station?"

"We could start with that."

"Great! Thank you!"

As I start heading for Glen Palmer's office, he says, "Dani?"

I turn to face him.

He says, "Palmer doesn't like you."

"I know."

He pauses a moment, then says, "Congratulate him."

"For what?"

"He just got promoted to Captain, Level 1."

"Really?"

"Really. But he turned it down."

"Why?"

"He wants to solve the Kern case."

"Really? Wow! I never realized Palmer was that dedicated."

"Me either, but here's the thing: they're gonna hold the position for him till he's ready. Can you believe it? Pretty damn impressive, if you ask me."

"I agree. Thanks, Frank."

"This is just a gesture of good faith, Dani. Doesn't make us friends."

"I know. But it's a start."

I give him another smile, then remove my shoes and pad quietly to Lieutenant Palmer's office.

Chapter 16

"HEY GLEN!" I SAY CHEERFULLY.

He frowns. "I've been expecting you."

"Thanks. May I sit down?"

"No. You won't be here that long. What do you want?"

I study his face, wondering why my mere presence annoys him so much. After all, I'm trying to help him. I start off with: "I know you questioned Abbey Rayne in connection with Tommy Kern's murder."

"You *know* that, huh? Should I be impressed? I'm not. Just proves you watch TV."

"You might remember that Abbey's my former client, from back when Tommy Kern raped her."

"Allegedly."

I hold my temper. "Right. Her and the six other young ladies who came forward over an 18-month period. Anyway, Abbey asked me something you should know before crossing her off your suspect list."

"Doesn't matter. She didn't do it. She was at a 24-hour dance-a-thon when the murder took place."

"I know, but—"

"She danced nonstop, in front of hundreds of people, with different partners. She never left the dance floor."

"Have you ruled out a hitman?"

He rolls his eyes.

"I'm serious, Glen."

"Lieutenant Palmer."

"Right. Sorry."

He says, "I already know about the hitman."

"You...*what?*"

"Six months ago she asked if you knew a hitman she could hire to kill Tommy. You told her you didn't, and she never asked again."

"How could you possibly—"

She told me. Said you were gonna come here and tell me the same story. It's the reason I was expecting you."

"She volunteered that information about the hitman?"

"Why not? She's got nothing to hide."

"You checked it out somehow?"

"Three things: one, she has no money. We checked her bank records. Two, there are no suspicious calls on her phone. Three, twenty-seven stab wounds? That's no hitman."

"What if the hitman did that to throw you off?"

"He'd never get another job. And anyway, where's this kid gonna find a hitman?"

"You checked her cell phone records?"

"Nope. We checked her *actual* phone and laptop."

I do a double-take. "Her attorney let you *have* them?"

He smiles. "She didn't request an attorney."

"Why not?"

"Who cares? But she *did* mention you warned her about talking to the police, and how we're a bunch of fucking liars."

"Uh..."

"Don't bother denying it. I'd trust her word over yours any day."

I'm stunned and hurt. Why would she tell him that?

As if reading my mind he says, "I think she was pissed you felt obligated to rat her out about the hitman. You lost her trust."

I look at him. "Can I ask *you* a question?"

"Make it quick."

"Why don't you like me?"

"You really want to know?"

I nod.

"You break the rules."

"I get results."

"Yes you do. By breaking the law."

"That's not...*entirely* true."

"Oh really? You deny hacking into computers and breaking into houses to gather evidence?"

"Yes."

"Then add liar to the list of things I dislike about you."

I sigh. "I'd like to be friends."

"With who?"

I smile. "You, of course!"

"Not gonna happen."

"I'm sorry I've given you the wrong impression about me, and I'm sorry for what I said about the police when I spoke to Abbey. But I bet you'd advise your own daughter not to talk to the police without an attorney."

"I don't have a daughter."

"Oh. Well, if you were advising a friend or relative?"

"Are we done here?"

"I'm willing to help."

"Excuse me?"

"If you need any help with the investigation, I'm available. For free, of course."

He looks at me like I'm Hitler with a microwave. Nothing left but to pull out my secret weapon, my Hail Mary. So I look him in the eye and say: "I was very impressed to hear you turned down the promotion to Captain, and especially *why* you did it. That shows amazing dedication on your part."

His ears, neck, and face turn bright red. "Is that supposed to be a *joke?*"

"What do you mean?"

"Lieutenant *Barbour* got the promotion, not me. He turned it down, and they're holding it for him. *Holding* it for him while he solves his *own* bullshit case!"

"But—"

"Get the *fuck* out of my office!" he snarls.

Chapter 17

ACCORDING TO THE MEDIA...

Here's what we know about the Tommy Kern murder:

1. It occurred in the basement of his fraternity house, which happens to be the same basement where he raped Abbey Rayne six months ago.

2. He was stabbed 27 times, and his body wasn't found for at least an hour after the attack.

3. He was fully clothed during the attack.

4. No one saw him go into the basement, or if they did, they're not admitting it.

5. No one saw him with a girl that night, or if they did, they're not admitting it.

6. The police have interviewed most, if not all the fraternity brothers.

7. The investigation is ongoing.

Part Two: Abbey Rayne

Chapter 1

Two Weeks Earlier...

ABBEY APPLIES A HENNA tattoo to her right wrist, a fake mole to her left cheek, then dons the wig, glasses, and the nondescript outfit she keeps hidden in the wheel well of her mini SUV. After looping a small messenger bag over her left shoulder, she drives to the shopping mall, removes her bike from the back seat, and rides four miles to the convenience store near Chad and Susie Dawkins's house.

She places her bike in the bike rack, chains her wheels, and walks the final mile to their front door. Now, on the porch, she rings the doorbell and waits, then rings it again.

The door opens, and a pleasant, middle-aged woman says, "May I help you?"

"Mrs. Dawkins, I need to speak to you and your husband."

Susie Dawkins frowns. "Whatever you're selling, we're not interested."

"I'm not selling anything. This is about Seth."

"What about him?" Susie can't help glancing at Abbey's bosom and stomach, to see if she's pregnant.

Abbey smiles. "It's nothing like that. In fact, I don't even *know* Seth. Not personally, anyway."

Susie relaxes a bit. "*Who* are you?"

"Sybil Gray. I'm a student at the college."

Susie looks confused. "And *why* are you here?"

"Seth's having an issue at school."

"What sort of issue?"

"I'd rather not discuss it on your doorstep, but there's been an incident. Something I can help you with."

"Seth hasn't mentioned any incidents."

"I wouldn't expect him to. But he's gotten into trouble, and it's about to blow up on him big time. May I join you?"

Susie sets her jaw. "I think not." She starts to close the door, but a voice behind her says, "Let her in, Suze. It can't hurt to hear what she's got to say."

Susie stares at Abbey a moment, then steps aside to let her enter.

"Thank you Mr. Dawkins. I'm only here to help."

"I doubt that," Susie says.

Abbey stifles a smile, takes a seat in the comfy chair, waits for them to sit on the sofa. When they do, Chad says, "What's this about, Sybil?"

Abbey says, "I'll start by telling you something we all know: your son's a rapist."

Chapter 2

"I BEG YOUR PARDON!" Susie says, feigning outrage. But Chad doesn't bother going through the motions. He simply asks, "What's happened now?"

"Thanks for remaining calm. I'm only here to help."

"Has there been...a claim?"

"You mean *another* claim? Not yet."

"Then...what are you trying to say?"

"Last Saturday night Seth drugged and raped a young lady named Bryn Wilder. She's eighteen, and comes from a wealthy family."

"I'd prefer you not use the word rape in connection with our son," Chad says. "It's not only repugnant, but inaccurate, since rape at the college level is so difficult to define."

"Is it?"

"Let's just say sexual misunderstandings are commonplace among coeds."

"I agree. Especially when it comes to Seth. But no matter, I'll get right to the point: Bryn Wilder's on the fence
about pressing charges. But I can talk her out of it...in return
for $25,000."

Susie lunges at Abbey, but Chad restrains her.
Surprisingly, she slaps *his* face! Twice!

He grabs her wrists. "Stop it, Suze! You're making
things worse."

She yells, "If you think I'm going to let this bitch come
into our house and—"

Abbey holds up her hand. "I'm trying to be nice here,
Suze, but I don't have to be."

Chad says, "We're obviously not going to pay you, and
I'll tell you why: Seth is what most college girls consider
quite a catch. He's handsome, popular, and financially secure, which often works to his detriment when dating
young, impressionable ladies. Yes, there have been a couple
of allegations by spurned, jealous girlfriend wannabees, but
none have amounted to a prosecutable case."

Susie chimes in: "We're actually considering suing those
little whores."

"Of course you are," Abbey says, dryly. "But here's the
thing, *Chad*: This case is different. And I can make it go
away for twenty-five grand, or you can take your chances in
court."

"These cases never go to court."

"This one will."

"So you say." He steeples his fingers and says, "Humor
me. What's so special about *this* one?"

Abbey opens her bag, removes a thumb drive. "This particular rape has been captured on video."

Susie says, "Take it from her!"

Chad looks at his wife. "Surely you know there's another copy." He turns to Abbey and says, "We'll obviously want to view it."

"I'm glad to let you," Abbey says, "but if I do, the price doubles."

"*Excuse* me?"

"You can trust me right now for $25,000, or pay me $50,000 after watching the video. But know this: if I'm not paid in full by Thursday morning at ten, the video goes to Bryn Wilder's parents. I think you can assume they'll go after Seth with guns blazing."

"Is Bryn Wilder behind this shakedown?"

Mockingly, Abbey says, "I'd prefer you not use the word shakedown in connection with this financial transaction. It's not only repugnant, but inaccurate, since shakedowns are so difficult to define."

"Very funny, Miss Gray. Fine, call it what you want. Is Miss Wilder behind it?"

"No. She has no clue about the video. If she did, Seth would already be in jail."

"So we're supposed to believe you somehow taped Seth and this Bryn character having sex," Susie says. She looks at her husband. "I'll tell you what's going on: this girl and Bryn Wilder got together and set Seth up. Bryn faked the rape and they're going to split the blackmail payment."

Chad shakes his head. "I don't think so. This one's acting far too smug about the video." Addressing Abbey, he says, "You're really enjoying this, aren't you."

"Does it show?"

"I'll give you a little warning, Sybil," he says, then smiles, wryly. "That's not your name, though, is it?"

Abbey says nothing.

Chad says, "You're floating high in the pond right now, but remember this: what goes around, comes around."

"Oh, does it *ever!*" Abbey says.

Chad works to control his anger. "Let's talk details. I give you the money, *then* what?"

"I destroy this video and the copies."

"Copies? Plural?"

"There are three."

"I assume we have to take your word for that?"

"I'm afraid so."

"And what proof would we get that you won't return for additional payments?"

"None. You'll have to trust me. But..." She looks into his eyes. "You absolutely *can* trust me to do everything I say, whether I'm making a threat or a promise." She adds, "And this is a two-way street, because what prevents you from calling the cops, or letting them ambush me when I come to collect the balance?"

"I suspect you've got that covered. Someone else is involved, someone who'll make the video public. Not that my attorneys wouldn't be able to convince a judge it was recorded illegally."

Abbey says, "If you rat me out, I might do prison time. But if this video goes public Seth's future will be ruined. I'm playing the high-risk game of hoping you love your son more than you hate paying me twenty-five grand."

"Fifty."

"Does that mean you want to see the video?"

"You know I have to."

Susie says, "You're the worst type of scum to treat us this way. We're his *parents*! We didn't do anything wrong! Why don't you just tell the truth: you don't give a shit about us! You come in here saying you want to help? Bullshit! You're here because we have the ability to pay, pure and simple. But as bad as that is, you're actually *teasing* us. You'll extort $25,000 for an accusation or charge us twice that to view your video? Well, fuck you!"

Abbey says, "You're looking at it completely backwards, Mrs. Dawkins. I know you love your son, just as my parents love me. But of course I'd rather get $50,000. That's the price, after all. I'm only offering you this huge discount so you won't have to see what a monster your son really is."

"We'll watch the video," Chad says, solemnly.

"You're sure?"

"Leave it with us. We'll watch it and get back to you."

Abbey laughs. "Do I look like Sonny Wortzik to you?"

"Who's that?" Susie says.

"The guy Al Pacino played in *Dog Day Afternoon*. I'm not naïve. If you want to see what Seth did, I'll show you. But you'll place your phones where I can see them at all times, and I control the thumb drive." She looks around. "So. You ready to do this?"

Chad nods.

"Where's your computer?"

Chapter 3

IN THE VIDEO, Bryn Wilder is clearly staggering as Seth leads her into the basement.

"She's clearly drunk," Susie says.

"Your point?"

"That won't look good in court."

"Hold that thought," Abbey says.

"I notice she's not protesting," Chad says.

He's right, Bryn's saying very little. But that changes when Seth tries to remove her clothes. She resists, and he says, "Don't be like that, sweet thing. You *know* you want it!" She tells him no, repeats herself, tells him to please stop, then screams, and tries to get away. But he grabs her shoulders and slams her head against the concrete wall. Not hard enough to crush her skull, but hard enough to daze her.

"Seth's version of getting a girl's consent," Abbey says.

Bryn's knees buckle, and she starts sliding down the wall to the floor. She's practically unconscious, but Seth lands a hard punch to her face for good measure, then drags her to the center of the room, and rolls her onto her stomach. He pulls her pants down and...things go from bad to worse. The rape is vicious, horrific, and lasts nearly ten minutes. Afterward, Seth hears someone hollering his name, so he throws sheets and blankets over Bryn's body and threatens to kill her if she makes a sound. He calls up the stairs to his friend that he's smoking a joint and will be up shortly, but the friend says, "You're not fooling anyone, Seth. Let me know when you're done. I want a turn." Seth calls out, "Are you alone?" The guy says, "Yeah." Seth tells him to come on down. He does, and when he comes into view, Susie gasps, "Omigod! That's *Paul*!"

"Shut up!" Chad says.

"It's okay," Abbey says. "Paul's parents have already paid."

Chad and Susie's eyes go wide.

"They've *seen* this?" Chad says.

"Of course not. That would betray Seth's privacy. I showed them a different rape featuring Paul, acting alone."

"By telling us that, you're betraying *Paul's* privacy."

"Can't help it. This is the only rape video I have on Seth. I could have edited Paul out of it, but I wanted you to see their interaction because it proves they've done this before with other girls. It makes the previous allegations against Seth part of the evidence package."

Meanwhile, on the video, Seth says, "If you want a turn you'll have to help me get her upstairs and go with me to dump her in Fuck Gulch."

"Won't be the first time," Paul says.

"Or the last!" Seth says, with a laugh.

Bryn begs them to let her go, and tries to hit them, but she's flailing her arms in slow motion. They laugh at her, and Paul takes his turn. Then Seth does her again while Paul watches. Paul wants another go, but can't get it up, so he curses Bryn and slaps her across the mouth as if it's her fault he can't make it happen. Then they put her clothes back on, prop her arms over their shoulders, and walk her out of the room toward the stairs.

The screen goes black, Abbey removes the thumb drive from the computer and says, "I'll need the money in fifties and twenties."

"I don't have fifty grand," Chad says.

"Don't insult me," Abbey says. "I came up with that number because it represents a year's tuition. If necessary, Seth can sit out a year. That should prevent at least two more rapes."

"I didn't finance his education. He got a student loan."

Abbey smiles. "If that's true, you've got even more cash than I thought. But I'm not here to gouge you. Think of it this way: you can pay me $50,000 to make this go away or you can pay your attorney twice that to defend Seth in a criminal case. Except that your attorney's going to lose."

"Despite what you think, I can't get that much cash by Thursday."

"Yes you can, Chad, and you will. You already told me Seth is quite the catch. You said he's handsome, popular, and financially secure, and those qualities often work to his detriment. Try to imagine how popular those same qualities will make him in prison. Pay the money, Chad. Because if you don't I absolutely *will* give this video to Bryn Wilder's parents. And before you look for a loophole, let me assure you, Bryn did the full rape kit at Cassidy Center within two hours of the assault, so all that evidence is sitting there, waiting for her to say yes to criminal charges. The only thing holding her back is she's not convinced she has enough proof of rape to get a conviction. But with this video evidence..."

Chad sighs. "Wait here."

"You're not going to *pay* her!" Susie says.

"I can either pay her or kill her," Chad says, "But saving fifty grand isn't worth a life sentence in prison, and it won't save Seth. This bitch's accomplice would turn the video over to the cops and Bryn's parents."

Abbey nods. "Well said, Chad."

He leaves the room and surprises Abbey by returning with two items: a thick bundle of cash, and a handgun, which he points at her chest.

"You know what this is?" he says, cocking the hammer.

If he's trying to scare her it's not working. She says, "Looks like a .357 magnum, with a set of Hogue rubber Monogrips. If you don't mind my saying so, your weapon's been seriously neglected. The barrel's scratched and the rear sight assembly's rusted. Why do you ask?"

"Because this is the gun that's going to blow your fucking head off if you come back for more money, or if I have reason to believe you failed to destroy the videos."

"You don't have to threaten me, Chad," she says, calmly. "You did your part, I'll do mine."

She holds her hand out to accept the cash, and he hands it over with slumped shoulders. She puts it in her bag and waits for him to lower his gun. When he does, she says, "I know you're furious, but you did the right thing. And if for some reason I can't talk Bryn out of prosecuting, I'll refund your money."

They follow Abbey to the front door. She opens it, and says, "Chad?"

He looks at her.

"A word of advice: tell Seth the next time he rapes a girl, turn the fucking lights off."

"*Fuck you!*" Susie shouts.

"Not today," Abbey says.

Chapter 4

THIS ISN'T HOW ABBEY planned to build her fortune. But like her business professor once said, you have to be able to adapt to changing circumstances. Have to seize the opportunities that come your way. Have to be willing to change your business model if your original one proves faulty.

Well, Abbey's business model was a complete bust. She worked hard, studied hard, joined all the right organizations, and performed endless hours of volunteer work. She'd been a high school National AP Scholar, a National Merit Finalist, and even won a prestigious citizenship award. No one could have been more prepared for college, and when the letter came in the mail offering her a full scholarship to her dream college she thought her heart would burst from the excitement. All her efforts had been rewarded, and she had no intention of resting on her laurels.

She worked even harder her first semester, and ended the year as one of only three finalists for the Outstanding Freshman Award. Didn't win it, but she *did* make the Dean's List all four quarters, which got her onto the President's List and put her on track to graduate summa cum laude.

Then, second week as a sophomore, she reluctantly attended a frat party where she was drugged, beaten, and raped by a very nice young man named Tommy Kern, an honors athlete who's biography made Abbey's look shabby by comparison.

She reported the rape. Endured the discomfort and humiliation of the rape kit. Met with her college counselor and was told: "You're facing an uphill battle."

"Why?"

"It's your word against his."

"Maybe so, but I'm the one with all the cuts and bruises."

"Can you prove he did that to you?"

"You think I'd do it to myself?"

"Had you been drinking?"

"Yes."

"Well, there you go. How many drinks did you have?"

"I consumed exactly one date rape cocktail."

"Can you prove that?"

"No."

"I notice you're not 21."

"Neither are you. What's your point?"

"You shouldn't have been drinking in the first place. You were breaking the law."

"Everyone in that frat house was drinking, and none of them were 21, far as I know."

"Maybe so, but they're not claiming to be raped."

"Are you saying the underage drinking law only applies to date rape victims?"

"I'm saying you purposely put yourself in a compromising situation."

"You're bringing up an interesting point," Abbey said. "How can frat houses serve drinks to underage college students? Last time I checked, even bars and restaurants aren't allowed to do that."

"Trust me, you don't want to bark up that tree."

"Why not?"

"The fraternity lobby is one of the biggest in Congress."

"They *must* be, if they're allowed to operate as unlicensed bars."

"That's a bit of a stretch."

"Is it? They're routinely serving liquor to minors, and doing so without a liquor license, and without checking ID's."

"You'll get nowhere with that argument. Let's talk about the clothes you wore."

"What difference does *that* make?"

"Mr. Kern's attorney will make it sound like you were dressed for a sexual encounter."

"I was dressed appropriately."

"One person's appropriate is another person's fantasy."

"Let me put it this way: I was dressed so appropriately my friends made fun of me."

"Can you describe what you were wearing?"

"Of course. But if you really care, you can go to the medical center and view them yourself, since they're part of the rape kit. I'll apologize in advance for the blood and semen stains."

"Your snarky attitude won't play well in court."

"Thanks for the advice. I'll make a point to curb my snark during the trial." She paused, then said, "I didn't come here today with this attitude. It's a defense mechanism against your total lack of concern."

"It may seem that way to you, but you have no idea how many young women walk in here each week claiming to have been raped."

"Maybe not, but I bet the prosecuting attorney would like to know. Because if it's only *one* girl a week it's one too many. And if it's *more* than one it speaks to an alarming lack of campus security."

"You didn't let me finish my comment. I was going to ask if you knew how many times we investigated girls who claimed rape but were found to be lying."

"I have no idea. But it can't possibly be all of them."

"You might be surprised. A girl drinks too much, engages in consensual sex, doesn't get asked out again, gets her feelings hurt, cries rape."

"Do these girls have cuts, bruises, black eyes and busted lips?"

"Sometimes. But that doesn't prove they were caused by the young man in question."

"Are you advising me not to take Tommy Kern to court?"

"Yes. Unless you're prepared to tell a packed courtroom every detail of every sexual encounter you've ever had. Because if you take him to trial, your entire sexual history will be a matter of public record."

"You might be interested to know that apart from this rape, my sexual history is practically nonexistent."

"Maybe so, maybe not. But here's what I *do* know: right now you're angry."

"Ya think?"

"You might be angry for all the right reasons, or because you granted Mr. Kern sexual favors and he moved along to another conquest. Either way, this is a major, life-changing decision. You've already done the rape kit, so the evidence is there whenever you decide to pursue it. Knowing that, I think you should go home, give this situation a lot of thought, see how you feel in a few days."

Abbey couldn't believe what she was hearing. "I'll tell you what's wrong with that plan," she said. "Tommy Kern's a rapist. If he can rape me and get away with it, what's to stop him from raping someone else while I'm sitting at home, giving it some thought?"

"If you insist on taking this to court, you'll almost certainly lose. And if you fail to win a conviction, you'll probably lose your scholarship as well."

"Are you being serious right now?"

"It's happened before."

"Sounds like you're threatening me."

"It's my duty to let you know the consequences of making false accusations."

"Making a false accusation isn't the same as losing in court."

"You should save that argument for the committee."

"I'm not just trying to get justice, I'm trying to protect the next girl. I only wonder why *you're* not." She added, "I'm really disappointed in you. Last year you said I could always come to you with my problems. And here I am, with the worst problem imaginable, and you don't even care! I believed in you. *Trusted* you! And trusted the school I've loved my whole life."

After that meeting, things went downhill quickly.

Abbey pursued the rape charge, but the case fizzled for lack of proof. One of the mistakes she made was hiring Dani Ripper, a local private detective, who discovered Tommy Kern had been accused of raping six other coeds over the prior eighteen months. While that was valuable information, it was obtained illegally by her teenaged partner, an accomplished computer hacker. The college nearly sued Ms. Ripper and her associate for the unauthorized access, but eventually backed away, fearing the public might focus on the information rather than the hack, specifically the part where they allowed a six-time accused rapist to remain on campus as a full-time student.

As for Abbey? They pulled her scholarship, effective the end of the current semester.

Hence the need to adapt her business model to her changing circumstances.

So here she is, driving to Luke and Nina Parish's home in Atlanta, preparing to tell them about a video recorded in the basement of a frat house in a small college in Missouri, where their son is enrolled as a chemical engineer. Same subject, different family, different college, different victim. All told, Abbey placed recording equipment in four fraternity houses: one local, two in Missouri, one in Illinois. In each place she picked the frat house with the worst reputation.

The first one was simple, since she knew the lay of the land. After all, she'd been raped there. She attended their next party and snuck down to the basement before the first assault took place. The room was so full of junk she didn't need to work hard to hide her equipment. She was in and out in two minutes, max.

The next ones weren't so easy.

As a good-looking young lady, crashing out-of-state frat parties was simple. But getting into the basements to set up her hidden camera required a foolproof plan, so she came up with one that worked every time. She'd get to the parties early, flirt with one of the frat guys, ask if they could go somewhere to take things to the next level.

The boys were happy to oblige.

Once in the basements, they'd start pawing her, and she'd say, "I'm really into this, but if you want me to go all the way you'll have to fetch me a really strong drink." That comment would send them running upstairs, giving her time to not only place her camera, but sneak back up the stairs and out the door.

The cameras have battery packs good for 80 hours of motion-detected activity that Abbey figures is roughly equivalent to two months of filming. The cameras record directly to her laptop, so she can review them at her leisure.

Biggest surprise so far?

Most of the sex she's recorded was consensual.

That said, in just under four weeks she's recorded 22 actual rapes, 9 of which were horrific. And these are the ones she's monetizing.

By 7:00 p.m. she's sitting at the kitchen table with Luke and Nina Parish, saying: "Did you know that 25% of all girls who attend college will be sexually assaulted before graduating?"

"That can't possibly be true," Nina says. "But what's that got to do with Mark?"

"It *is* true, and it's a statistic common to colleges throughout the nation. And the amazing thing? The vast majority of these rapes are caused by only 8% of the male students: repeat offenders like your son, Mark. The colleges turn a blind eye and let them remain on campus, knowing they'll continue assaulting coeds. Can you guess why?" She pauses, then says, "The colleges can't afford to admit the problem exists because parents would never send their daughters to a college where they face a one-in-four chance of being sexually assaulted, and boys won't attend colleges where girls are scarce. So any college that admits they have serious rape problems will lose a ton of tuition money, as well as alumni funding. Because who wants their giving associated with a rape scandal? I'm not saying the colleges are *eager* to sacrifice their female students for funding, but they're certainly *willing* to."

Luke says, "I don't appreciate you lumping Mark into this equation. There's absolutely no proof that he—"

Nina interrupts, saying, "For God's sake, he's got a *girlfriend!*"

Abbey looks at her incredulously, then begins her spiel about how they can pay her $25,000 now, or $50,000 after watching the video of Mark raping Lexi Siegel. Like the others, Luke and Nina want to see the video. When it ends, Luke says he can give her $200 tonight, and the rest in a few days.

Will he call the cops?

She doubts it, but then again, you never know. So she says, "I'll trust you for the rest, but I'll need some collateral."

"Like what?" Luke asks.

"A printout of all your email contacts."

"Why?"

"If I suspect a trap, or fail to get paid by ten a.m. Thursday, my associate will blast Mark's rape video to every man, woman, and child on your email list."

"Sorry," Luke says. "That's unacceptable."

She returns his $200. "Sorry you feel that way. Good evening."

"*Wait!*" Nina says. "What are you going to do?"

Abbey presses a button on her phone. Then says, "Luke and Nina declined our offer. Go ahead and send the video to Lexi's parents...That's right, then post it on Mark's personal Facebook Page, then Nina's...No, I realize Mark hasn't been on Facebook for months. But he's got 200 followers who'd love to see it. And be sure to post it on YouTube. They'll remove it in about four hours, but the damage will be done...yeah, do it now."

"*Wait!*" Nina says. "We'll give you the lists. And the cash."

Abbey covers the phone. "You've got the cash here?"

"No," Luke says. "But I'll have it by Thursday. Or at least half of it."

Abbey bites the corner of her lip. "I'll need the full $50k by 10 o'clock Thursday morning, Luke. If you can't get the full amount, tell me now."

Like Chad before him, Luke's shoulders are slumped, his hands shaking. "Okay."

Abbey gets back on the phone and says, "They're back on board. You haven't posted the video yet, have you?" There's a short pause. "Fuck." She ends the call, looks at Luke and Nina. "I'm sorry. It's done."

Nina's face turns white. "What are you saying?"

"My guy already posted the video. It's...everywhere."

Nina faints. Luke tries to catch her, but he's so busy retching, he loses his grip and she falls to the floor. Abbey says, "When she wakes up, tell her I was kidding. Nothing's been sent. Not yet, at least. But come Monday morning, when the banks are open, try to remember how you felt just now, and let that feeling guide the decisions you make between now and 10 o'clock Thursday morning. Because I *will* burn your son if you try to fuck me over."

She takes his $200 and leaves their home feeling confident about next week's meeting. She walks to her bike in the dark, rides it to the hotel where she parked her car, loads it into the back seat and drives to a different hotel, then gets a room. Once there, she showers, orders room service, and reviews the thumb drive she'll show Jeff and Margo Taylor tomorrow morning, assuming they're home when she comes to call. Their palatial estate is located less than 60 miles from downtown Atlanta, and this visit should be interesting, since their son, Sterling, is the worst of the bunch.

Being Friday night, Abbey figures the four cameras will get a lot of action. She checks her friendly neighborhood frat house first, and is shocked to find two boys going at it hot and heavy, a first for her cameras. Knowing the boys, she watches with interest to make sure the sex is consensual, since 4% of all male college students also get raped while in school, and...whoa! Are you *kidding*?

Omigod!

Yes! *Definitely* consensual!

She fast-forwards through the rest of that one and spends the next hour casually reviewing the others, until it dawns on her she's witnessed so many violent acts she's become desensitized to even the most brutal rapes.

Abbey falls asleep depressed and wakes up in a funk. She showers, puts on her disguise, checks out, and heads to Jeff and Margo's estate.

Chapter 5

THE TAYLORS OFFER $5,000 DOWN and hope to have the balance by Thursday, ten a.m.

Would a drug dealer cut them this much slack? Would a contract killer take so little down? Abbey wonders if she's being too easy on them. She asks for a printout of their email contacts, and Jeff and Margo provide them so quickly she doesn't have to make a fake call to her imaginary associate.

That's not to say her threats of exposure aren't real.

They're quite real!

If Abbey's arrested, her first phone call will be to her friend, Cameron Reeder, at which time she'll tell Cameron where to find the pre-stamped envelopes she's prepared. Cameron will put the letters in the nearest mailbox, and that will be that.

The envelopes contain a short note describing what the recipients will find on the enclosed thumb drives, and will be sent unedited to the police, the victims and their parents, and the local TV outlets in each of the four college towns. Each thumb drive will include all the rapes that took place in that particular frat house.

That should shake things up!

Since Abbey won't immediately know which parent turned her in to the police, she'll burn them all, including the parents who paid her. It'll be all or nothing, a scorched-earth policy to ensure Abbey won't be the only one doing prison time.

This is not who Abbey is...but it's who she's become.

She's done her homework: it's true that colleges and universities allow known rapists to remain on campus un-punished, and for this reason there's no ground more fertile for budding rapists to cultivate their skills. Though you'll never see these details on a college brochure, you'd hope during the new student safety orientation the girls would be told that 300,000 college women experience sexual assault each year, and drugs and alcohol are the main factors. They should mention 85% of the girls will know their attacker prior to the assault, and that 15% of the assaults will involve gang rape. They should tell the girls that 70% of gang rape perpetrators belong to fraternities, and 86% of off-campus sexual assaults occur at frat houses. They should warn the girls that 4% of all rape victims were given drugs without their knowledge, and that the system is so stacked against them their attackers will have less than a 1 in 2,500 chance of being prosecuted and found guilty.

As for her advisor's claim that most of the girls were lying?

Not true.

The stats show less than 2% percent of female students lie about being raped.

Abbey's advisor was quick to discourage her from reporting the crime, and went so far as to threaten her scholarship. But that was the least significant threat Abbey received after reporting the crime. Since Tommy Kern was a starting player on the football team, her rape allegation nearly cost him playing time, which put her at odds with the entire student body. She received more than twenty death threats.

Death threats!

For telling the truth.

Abbey knows what she's doing to these parents is shitty. But what was done to her was far worse. She made the mistake of attending a party and wound up savagely beaten and raped. Tried to report it, but was discouraged, threatened, and lost the scholarship she'd worked so hard to earn, along with all hope of continuing her education.

Well, not *all* hope, since Abbey decided to adapt her business model to the changing circumstances. By the time she's finished with these parents she'll have no problem funding her own education and starting her own business.

She's not proud of building her future on the backs of beleaguered parents whose sons have raped other women. But on the other hand, if not for the parents, there'd be no rapists.

Chapter 6

Wednesday Evening.

ALTHOUGH ABBEY HAS COLLECTED the full $50,000 from six different parents without incident, these "come back Thursday" situations always feel like a trap. With each passing day the parents' outrage increases, even as their sense of danger decreases. She set up two meetings to collect the Atlanta area balances tomorrow morning at ten, but knows if they're planning to pay they'll have the money tonight. If either has contacted the police, she's likely to be the victim of a sting operation, but if so, Abbey figures the police will arrive first thing tomorrow morning, not tonight.

She knocks on Luke and Nina Parish's door at 7:45 p.m. and notes their shocked expressions. "I assume you have my cash?" she asks.

"You said tomorrow, ten o'clock," Luke says.

"So I did. But here I am."

"We don't have it yet."

"Why not?"

"We were going to the bank first thing tomorrow."

"You're lying. Why?"

"It's the truth!"

"You expect me to believe you waited four days to go to the bank, and only gave yourself an hour to withdraw $50,000 and get back home in time to give it to me?"

"It took a few days to get the money into the account."

"And is it in the account now?"

"Yes, of course."

"Sorry Luke. I think you're lying."

She removes a gun from her bag. "Let's go to your car."

Luke and Nina go through all the motions of disbelief and protest she expected, but when she cocks the hammer, they do as they're told. She gets the keys to Nina's car, leads them to the garage, and tells Luke to put his hands behind his back. Then she gives Nina a plastic zip tie and tells her to place it around his wrists. She does so, and Abbey says, "Make it tighter."

She does.

Then Abbey has her add a second one, and forces Luke into the trunk, and closes it.

"What're you going to do?" Nina says.

"Kill him, of course."

Nina does the whole begging and pleading thing, and eventually takes Abbey to the cash. Abbey puts the money in her bag, zip ties Nina's hands behind her back, puts her in the back seat of the car, places a giant plastic garbage bag over her head and forces her to lie down on the floor of the backseat. She grabs several armfuls of clothes from their closet and dumps them over Nina to conceal her from view. Then she drives Nina's car eight miles, pulls off the highway onto a long, overgrown road that eventually leads to an abandoned farmhouse, where she says, "Nina, call me a cunt."

From under the stack of clothes Nina's muffled voice says, "What?"

"You're angry, right? So tell me how you feel. Call me names. Cuss me out. Threaten me."

"I-I don't understand."

"You and Luke lied to me, tried to fuck me over. But now that I've been paid, I have no further use for either of you. All the way out here I've been telling myself the smart move is to kill you. But I've never killed anyone, and it's gonna take more than logic to make it happen. So if you'll be kind enough to threaten or insult me, it'll make my job a lot easier."

"Please. We want to live."

"Then you shouldn't have tried to set me up with the cops!"

"Wh-what are you *talking* about?"

Abbey looks at her gun, wonders if she has the guts to shoot them. She takes a moment to visualize how it would go down, and decides she can't. The problem is Luke. If they were both in the back seat she could probably do it. But if she shoots Nina, Luke would know he's next, and it would probably take at least a second shot to make sure Nina's dead. She'd be screaming, and begging, and bleeding, and...

Then she'd have to get out of the car, open the trunk and shoot Luke two or three times. Again, blood, begging, and screaming. Of course, she could try to get them out of the car and make them lie down on the ground so she could shoot them quickly, execution style. But it's dark, and they'll almost certainly try to run away. If she shoots and misses she'll have to hunt one or both of them down, and someone might hear the shots and find her before she can kill them both.

It's just too much.

So she says, "If you want to live, you'll need to do exactly as I say. Understood?"

She hears a muffled "Yes."

"We're just outside Atlanta on a farm road, half a mile from the highway. I'm gonna get out of your car, walk to mine, and drive away. When I get 200 yards from your car I'll put your keys in the center of the road, then get back in my car and honk the horn. When you hear the horn, you can get up and walk to the keys. But until I honk that horn you're not gonna move or make a sound. I'll be backing my car away from you with my headlights on, so if you try to get up, I'll see you. If you try to open your car door, the light will come on and I'll see you. Again, when I honk the horn, you're free to get up and search for your keys."

"How will I get my hands free?"

"Listen to this sound."

She drops something metallic into the plastic tray between the front seats. "Grooming scissors," she says.

Abbey gets out of Nina's car, walks 50 yards to her own car, and drives to the highway without bothering to honk her horn. Thinking, *Let them stew all night, they deserve it.*

So fucking sad it had to come to this.

Luke and Nina absolutely called the police and were planning a sting for tomorrow morning. Otherwise, why would they lie about having the money?

The bigger problem, of course, is the police know about the blackmail scam. They've probably alerted all the area banks, and possibly every bank in the state, which means she'll have to abort her plans to visit Jeff and Margo Taylor.

It's hard to pass up the chance to drive a mere 60 miles to get another fifty grand, but Abbey's a firm believer that too much greed will bring you down.

It's over.

She's disappointed, but safe. Yes, it sucks knowing everything's in place to video a couple dozen more rapes before the batteries run out on the recording equipment, as that could have brought her a million bucks. Still, she pocketed $350,000 cash in a matter of weeks, and dodged a major bullet tonight, so it's not all bad.

Now all she has to do is retrieve her bike from the elementary school where she stashed it, retrieve the camera equipment from the frat houses, and move on to the next phase of her life.

Chapter 7

Friday Evening.

THIS WOULD HAVE BEEN the perfect weekend to retrieve the cameras from the frat house basements, but
Abbey's stuck at Thon for the next 24 hours. Thon being
the annual dance marathon held in the student athletic center. She'd back out of her pledge in a heartbeat if she could,
but as co-chairman of the event, that's pretty much
impossible.

The way it works, girls from several sororities have
agreed to dance 24 hours nonstop with frat boys who paid
$10 per hour for the privilege of dancing with the girls of
their choice, provided the girls' dance cards have openings.
Of course, Abbey figures to dance alone or with girlfriends
all night, since she's been shunned by the entire frat com-
munity for crying rape last semester.

Which is why she's stunned when Cameron presents her dance card containing 24 names.

"That can't be mine!" Abbey says, surprised to hear excitement in her voice.

"Why not?" Cam says. "There are lots of fraternities here, and most frat guys are nice."

Is it possible some or several decent guys have found her?

Abbey accepts the card and checks the names...then chides herself for thinking things had changed. The names are all phony: Sponge Bob, Bart Simpson, Chuckie, Freddie, Straw Dog, and the like.

WTF?

When the music starts and the first guy approaches, it becomes evident what's going on: the usual suspects, the bastards, have signed up for the sole purpose of being able to threaten and insult her for an entire hour each, knowing she has no option but to listen to them, one after another, for 24 hours.

Lovely.

As the evening gets underway, her dance partners mock her during the fast dances and whisper threats and insults during the slow ones. Her third partner turns out to be Colson Ford, who played both pitcher and catcher with Jason Dennis on the gay sex video that popped up on her laptop last weekend. He starts by sneering, "Heard you lost your scholarship and have to quit college. Maybe you can find a career at Wendy's." From there it gets worse: "It's eight o'clock. Been raped yet?" And finally: "Tommy said you had the softest chin he ever laid his balls on."

Abbey does her best to ignore him, but when he says, "By the way, have you figured out which of the names on your dance card is Tommy?"—her knees buckle, and she almost goes down for the count. Having to dance with her rapist would be the absolute worst, especially during the slow dances. Seeing the panic in her eyes, Colson laughs and says, "I'll give you a hint: he'll be here before midnight!"

She doesn't need the hint. The name on her dance card says it all:

Straw Dog.

—Which she now realizes is a reference to the 1970s movie where Dustin Hoffman's wife, Susan George, gets brutally gang raped. The movie's popular in film school because of the controversy: halfway through the rape, Susan's character starts enjoying it. Like most coeds, Abbey hates the film because it feeds into the rapist mentality that says: "Don't pay attention to her protests. All women have rape fantasies. Your persistence will be rewarded. After a few minutes, she's going to love it."

Abbey fights the urge to vomit. More than anything, she'd love to punish Tommy for ruining her life. But she'd also love to say something to wipe that stupid smirk off Colson's face. Ideally, there'd be something she could say or do to punish both of them at the same time.

And then it hits her: the perfect idea.

She says, "Hey Colson: who are *you* dating these days?"

He puffs up. "Everyone, sweetheart! Including your girlfriends!"

Her smirk throws him off guard. He says, "What, you don't *believe* me?"

"Not at all."

"Ask around."

"Okay. I'll start with Jason."

That catches his attention. "*Who?*"

Abbey's turn to laugh. She says, "Jason Dennis. Your fuck buddy."

His face blanches.

She says, "Wait: did you think it was a *secret?*"

"Wh-what are you *talking* about?"

Colson's staring at her like she can't possibly know about this, but when she adds, "You and Jason in the frat house basement? Last weekend? Surely you remember!"

He sputters, "That's *bullshit!*" But he appears ready to faint.

Abbey hammers the final nail in his coffin: "Tommy Kern told me all about it."

Colson stops dancing. His eyes are wide with fear. "Wh-What did he say?"

"Just that he put a camera in the basement of your frat house and caught you and Jason fucking."

Colson's face morphs from frightened to furious. He shouts, "Fuck you!" and storms away.

Abbey hollers, "Thanks for the dance!"

Cameron Reeder rushes over. "What the *hell?* Are you *okay?*"

Abbey grins. "Never better!"

Two hours later Thon comes to an abrupt halt when a dozen kids come rushing in with the news that Tommy Kern has been murdered. Abbey and Cameron get caught up in the crowd pouring out into the street, and follow them to the frat house, where they wait behind crime scene tape for the body bag to be wheeled out. By then, thousands of students have clogged the street and surrounding yards.

The people around her fall into several camps: horrified, frightened, outraged. Someone behind her says, "It was just a matter of time."

She turns to find Colson ten feet away, staring directly into her eyes.

She grabs Cameron and says, "Let's go!"

"Where?"

"To celebrate."

"Omigod!" Cameron says. "You didn't just say that!"

Before they get thirty feet, Colson says, "Got a sec?"

Cameron comes to her defense, snarling, "Leave her alone, fuckwad!"

"Shut up, Dyke," he says, then looks at Abbey: "It'll just take a second. I promise."

Abbey says, "It's okay, Cam. Hang back, but keep me in sight, okay?"

Cameron nods.

Abbey follows Colson half a block till they get to a place they can speak privately. He says, "You were right about the camera equipment."

"You found it?"

"Yeah. And I destroyed it. But...I didn't kill Tommy."

"I'm pretty sure you did."

He shakes his head. "I wanted to, but he was already dead when I got there."

"You found the body?"

"No. A bunch of guys were in the basement when I got there. No one knows who did it."

"How'd he die?"

"He was stabbed to death. Like, I don't even *know* how many times."

"Did they find the murder weapon?"

"Yeah. In his chest. But wanna hear something *really* crazy? The cops found his shoes in the shower."

"What do you mean?"

"They were sopping wet."

"You're sure they were *Tommy's* shoes?"

"Yeah. His socks were next to his body, but not his shoes. That's crazy, right?"

Abbey looks at him. It's dark, but the nearby street light makes it possible to see his face. "You think Jason did it?"

"Of *course* not!" He goes quiet a moment. Then says, "I need to ask you something about the video."

"I told you what Tommy said. That's all I know."

"Who else could have seen it?"

"How should *I* know?"

"Did he tell anyone else?"

"I don't know. But I doubt it."

"You swear?"

"No. I mean, I *assume* he only told me."

"Why?"

"Because who could he have possibly told that wouldn't have said something to you or Jason by now?"

"Tommy Kern *hated* you."

"So?"

"So why would he tell *you* about the video?"

She shrugs. "I ran into him last week. He was drunk."

"What did he say, exactly?"

"He was verbally abusing me, like you guys always do. I tried to ignore him, but he kept fucking with me, and followed me out of the bar and said he had a video of us—me and him—having sex. He said he watches it whenever he's horny, and gets off on it. I called bullshit, and that's when he told me he hid a camera in the basement last semester and recorded dozens of guys having sex with their dates, including gang bangs. Then he said his camera even caught you and Jason going full oral and anal on each other. He was laughing about it."

"It's not true."

"No?"

"Never happened. I swear."

She shrugs again. "Okay. Whatever."

"You can't tell anyone about this."

"Why? Because you've been such a good friend to *me*?"

He looks down at his feet. "You've got every right to be pissed. I've treated you like crap. Everyone did. I mean, we nearly lost our *charter* because of all the stuff you were saying. And the other frat houses caught a lot of shit over it, too." He sighs. "I'm sorry for my part. But Abbey? This is my *life* right now. You've gotta *help* me!"

"What's the problem? You said you didn't do it. If that's true, you've got nothing to worry about."

"If you tell the police what Tommy said about the videos...they'll think I killed him."

From down the street, Cameron calls out, "Everything okay?"

"I'll just be another minute!" Abbey says. Then asks Colson, "What'd you do with the recording equipment?"

"Destroyed it. Threw it away."

"What about Tommy's computer?"

"Destroyed that, too."

"Did you watch the videos?"

"I couldn't. His computer was password protected. But I swear to God what he said about me and Jason wasn't true."

"Sorry. Don't believe you."

"Why not?"

"First of all, I couldn't care less if you guys are gay. What's the big deal?"

"We're jocks. You have no idea what that type of rumor could do to us."

She shakes her head. "You're making *way* too big a deal out of this. If you're gay you should just admit it and move on."

"I'm not gay."

"Fine. Whatever."

"You don't *believe* me? I've fucked half the girls you know!"

"That's a complete exaggeration, but I get your point. You like girls, not boys. But the fact remains, if Tommy lied about you and Jason, why'd you rush over to the frat house and destroy his computer and recording equipment?"

"Because I'm probably on those tapes. Not with Jason, but...certain girls."

"Girls you raped?"

"No. But..."

"Underage girls?"

"I don't know. Maybe. But if the police ever found those videos...it would be pretty bad for a lot of people. So I'm asking you: please don't tell anyone what I did, or what Tommy told you."

"I'll make you a deal: I won't say anything if *you* don't."

He looks surprised. "Why the fuck would *I* say anything?"

"You might tell Jason, and he might tell someone else. If someone tells the police, and they ask *me* about it, I'll have to tell them what I know. And if I understand correctly, you just confessed to destroying evidence in a murder case."

His voice rises an octave: "You can't prove that!"

"No, but I can tell my story and offer to take a lie detector test."

He grabs her arm. "Why would you *do* that?"

"Why would *you* spend an hour dancing with me just to threaten and humiliate me?"

"Because...I'm a jerk. But *you're* not."

"There are 1,800 fraternity guys on campus who'd argue that point."

"Not all of them. But yeah, probably most. And I was one of the worst. Look: I know I have no right to ask this favor, but if you don't help me, I'm fucked. But if you keep quiet about this I swear to God I'll make it up to you somehow. You want money? Five thousand dollars?"

She goes quiet a moment. "I'll tell you what I want, Colson: I want you to admit I was raped."

He sighs. "I know you were."

"I also want to know how many girls *you* raped in that basement."

"I didn't *rape* anyone."

"Wrong answer," she says, and turns to leave.

"Wait!"

She stops, turns to face him.

"Three," he says.

"Did any of them report you?"

"No."

"Fair enough."

He looks relieved. "Is that it? Are we good?"

"Not quite. I want you to admit you fucked Jason Dennis."

"I *didn't!* I swear to God."

"Then why do I smell dick on your breath?"

"*What? Fuck you!*"

"No chance."

She starts walking away.

He runs after her, grabs her arm. Cameron shouts, "Get the fuck away from her!" and starts running toward them. Abbey puts her hand up to stop her, then turns to Colson. "Why should I keep your secret if you won't even tell me the truth? Tommy videoed you with Jason and we both know it."

He looks around, then lowers his voice. "Okay, whatever. It's true. But it was just that one time. We were drunk, fooling around, things got out of hand."

"Say it. Out loud."

He pauses, looks around again, then says. "I fucked Jason Dennis."

"And?"

"He fucked me."

"Okay."

"Okay? What does that mean?"

"Your secret's safe with me."

"Swear to God?"

She nods. Then says, "Colson?"

"Yeah?"

"No means no."

"I know."

"Apparently, you don't. But after this, if I ever hear so much as a rumor that you forced yourself on someone—"

"You won't. I swear."

"Then we're good."

He breathes a huge sigh of relief. "Thank you."

"Have you told Jason any of this?"

"No. And I'm not going to."

"Good idea."

Abbey walks away with a spring in her step. She not only got Colson to murder Tommy, but he destroyed the recording equipment, as well.

Only two things left to do: (1) Find a secure hiding place for the cash, the envelopes with the thumb drives, and the secret laptop she used to receive the videos; and (2) Remove the hidden cameras from the other frat houses.

Cameron says, "What was *that* all about?"

"Can you *believe* it? He *apologized* to me. For all the shit he's done to make my life miserable."

"Sorry, I don't believe it."

"I think this whole Tommy thing gave him a new perspective." She stops short. "Would you do me a huge favor?"

"Name it."

"Can you call some friends to meet us at Dooley's so we can celebrate? And can you go there now and save me a seat?"

"Sure. What are *you* gonna do?"

"Finish the accounting for Thon and check to make sure the room's clean."

"Want some help?"

"Hell yeah! But after five hours of dancing, I'd rather have a good seat at Dooley's and some drinks, 'cause that place is gonna be *packed* tonight."

"Okay. But call if you need me."

"Thanks, Cam. You're a good friend."

Abbey watches her walk away, then heads to her sorority house, opens her locked drawer, removes one of her throwaway phones, presses a button. When a guy answers, she says, "Hey Toby, it's Abbey."

"Cool. What's up?"

"I need to ask you something, but it's serious, okay?"

"Okay."

"How far can I trust you?"

He pauses. "Is that the question?"

"Yes."

"What do you need?"

Chapter 8

ABBEY HAS A SECRET FRIEND. Not a boyfriend, but a lonely guy who'd love to have a relationship with her. Since that's not gonna happen, she's fortunate that he's willing to accept things as they are. But can she trust him to this degree? Probably not, but she needs to move quickly, since the police will undoubtedly want to question her about Tommy Kern. They'll seize her laptop and search her sorority house to see if they can locate his missing computer.

She says, "If I give you a box to hold for me, would you promise not to tell anyone?"

"Of course."

"Would you also promise not to open it?"

"Yes."

She pauses, then says, "You're the most honest person I know. But I can't imagine anyone being able to keep that promise. I certainly couldn't, if you asked me."

"I would never go through your things."

"Are you sure?"

"I won't open the box. You have my word."

Abbey smiles. She believes him.

She's not using Toby. Well, not leading him on, any-way. She's been clear from the start she's not interested in a physical relationship.

"How soon can we meet?" she asks.

He laughs. "I'm always available."

"How's right now?"

"Want me to come to you, or meet halfway?"

"Halfway. Starbucks. Fifteen minutes?"

"I'll be there in ten."

She smiles again.

Sure enough, when she turns into Starbuck's, there he is, standing in the parking space beside his car, saving a place for her, like they're kids in middle school, and it's lunch time. She pulls in, asks him to pop his trunk. When he does, she gives him the box and says, "Please don't let anything happen to this."

"I'll guard it with my life."

"And you won't look inside? Or let anyone else touch it?"

"I already promised that."

She smiles. "Yes you did. Thank you."

He laughs. "I've never seen a box with that much wrap-ping tape. It'd take a chain saw to get inside."

"That's my daddy's fault."

"What do you mean?"

"Daddy always said no matter how much you trust the dealer, always cut the cards."

"Good advice." He places it carefully in his trunk and says, "It's bigger than I expected."

The lights from the coffee shop and parking lot are crazy bright, and the place is doing lots of business. It suddenly occurs to her if someone saw her give a guy a box the night Tommy Kern was murdered—someone who knows her—it could create problems.

She looks into his eyes. "I won't forget this. If you ever need a favor from me, I'll promise to try."

"Maybe I'll give *you* something to hold," he says, smiling broadly.

Her expression changes instantly. "Was that meant to be sexual?"

Horrified, he says, "No! Of *course* not! I just meant...you know, you gave me a box, maybe I could give *you* one to hold. Doesn't matter what's in it. I just thought—"

Her expression softens. "Close your eyes," she says.

He does.

She gives him a quick kiss on the lips, then steps back.

He opens his eyes, and wide. "Wow!"

"That was a friendship kiss," she says.

"Oh no it wasn't!"

"Well, maybe not. But it wasn't a girlfriend kiss, either."

"True." He thinks a moment. "Does that mean we're somewhere in between?"

She smiles. "If you keep your promise about the box, then yes, that's exactly what it means."

"How long do you want me to keep it?"

"Does it matter?"

"No. I was just curious."

"I'll let you know."

They hug goodbye, and she drives to Dooley's to meet Cameron.

Chapter 9

ONLY TWO PEOPLE IN the world know who killed Tommy Kern...

And Abbey's one of them.

Yes, she packed her secret laptop in the box before heading to Starbucks, but not before checking the final recording.

The killer wasn't Colson Ford.

Wasn't Jason Dennis.

Wasn't a guy, a student, or a teenaged girl.

It was a woman Abbey had never seen before.

She didn't appear drunk or drugged, and seemed to have a plan from the moment Tommy led her into the basement, when she pointed at the mattress on the floor and said, "So this is where you take your little fresh-faced girl-friends and turn them into women?"

He laughed. "I told you it was dreadful."

She said, "I love it! Kiss me!"

"Really?"

"Uh huh."

They kissed, and she rubbed his crotch, and he felt her up, and she told him to lock the door. When he said it didn't lock, she reached into her bag and gave him some quarters and told him to wedge them into the space between the door and the frame to jam it shut.

Tommy said, "Does this mean we're gonna...?"

And she said, "Why else would I ask to see this foul little cellar?"

He said, "I don't know. But you're *way* too classy for this place."

"Am I?"

Abbey thinks so. The woman was possibly 40, great face, athletic body, a true MILF. She's wearing designer jeans, silk blouse, high-end heels.

Tommy said, "You deserve an expensive hotel room."

"Now you sound like my husband."

"Sorry."

"Don't be. It's a sweet thought. But can't you see everything about this is perfect?"

Tommy looked around. "Not really."

"I've had twenty years of polite sex in luxury hotels, and I'm sick of it. You know how long it's been since I've touched a hard dick? I want a young stud to fuck the shit out of me in a vulgar room on a filthy, cum-soaked mattress."

He frowned. "You're being sarcastic."

"Not in the least. If you'll wedge the door I'll get naked right now."

He stared at her. "Swear to God?"

"Need proof?" She took off her top, exposing her bra.

"Holy shit!"

"What?"

"Are those *real?*"

"You'll know in a minute."

"Omigod! You rock!"

"I'm just getting started. But fix the door, okay? I don't want to be standing here butt naked for the whole fraternity to see."

"No problem!"

"Don't peek till I tell you."

"Okay, but it won't be easy!"

"Good, because I like it hard!"

He pushed the quarters into the spaces till he felt they were secure. Then he pulled on the door to test it, but it flew open and the quarters scattered across the floor. He turned to face her, saw her in nothing but panties, and said, "Wow!"

"You weren't supposed to peek."

"Sorry. Couldn't help myself. By the way, nice abs."

"Thanks. Can you please fix the door now?"

"The quarters won't work," he said. "But seriously, there's nothing to worry about. No one's gonna be here for hours. They're all at the dance-a-thon."

"Whether they are or not, I'm not doing this unless the door's secure."

"I'll try again."

He picked up the quarters and tried again, and as he wedged them in place she removed her panties, pulled a chef's knife from her handbag, silently crossed the floor, and plunged it into his upper back as hard as she could. It went in so deeply she couldn't pull it out. He screamed and fell backward, onto the knife, which pushed it in even deeper, and as he writhed around she had to hop this way and that to avoid being kicked. After a time, she managed to get her hand around the handle, but Tommy's body was jerking so violently, she lost her grip. Finally she screamed something that struck Abbey as completely absurd, but it worked: "For God's *sake*," she said. "Let me *help* you!"

Tommy's brain was obviously scrambled, because how could he not know she's the one who stabbed him? But shockingly, he tried to hold still while she braced her bare foot against his back for leverage to pull the knife out.

"What happened?" he said. "What *happened?*"

"I can't get it out!" she said, frustrated.

Then she went back to her handbag and pulled out a small hatchet and when he saw it his eyes bugged out. "Remember Hailey?" she said. Without waiting for a response, she descended on him like a lumberjack trying to fell a giant tree. His eyes bugged out and he took two massive hits to his thigh before he could ball himself up to protect his torso. But she walked around him and started chopping everything between the hatchet and his heart. With blood flying in all directions he screamed, cried, begged her to stop, but she didn't even slow down. He tried to roll away, but that only pushed the knife deeper into his back, which caused him even more agony. He yelped and tried to fight back, but she was determined, and he was losing strength, and it was soon clear to Abbey he'd raped his last girl.

The carnage continued till she was finally convinced he was dead, at which point she made one last attempt to extract the chef's knife, to no avail. Then she did something that really surprised Abbey:

Chapter 10

SHE SAT BESIDE HIS body and stared at him.

With chest heaving, body shaking, she waited to catch her breath and regain her composure. If this had been Abbey, she would've hauled ass immediately. But this woman continued to sit there for several minutes, as if she had all the time in the world. Finally she got up, and this time—obviously having worked it out in her mind—rocked the knife back and forth to loosen it. Next time she pulled, it slipped out easily. She rolled him onto his back, then plunged the knife into the center of his chest, removed one of his shoes and socks and pushed the sock into his mouth like she was...

Actually, she was removing any saliva she might have left in his mouth from the kiss!

Then she used that same sock to wipe her palm prints from the knife handle. Finally, she swung her hatchet and made a deep chop into his crotch, which may or may not have severed his penis. Abbey couldn't tell, since he was fully dressed. Then she used the sock to wipe the blood around Tommy's body into a smear, and Abbey could only assume she was trying to hide her footprints, and the print her butt had made when she sat down.

Of course there was blood everywhere, including all over the woman's body, and Abbey had no clue how she planned to leave the scene without spreading even more blood. She knows that on TV the police can...

Wait.

Could it really be that simple?

The woman put Tommy's shoes on her feet, used his clean sock to wipe the wet blood from her hands, then casually walked to her handbag, removed a pair of gloves from it, placed the bloody hatchet back in the bag, then put the gloves on, picked up her clothes, removed the quarters from the door jamb, and walked out of the room completely naked, save for his shoes, her gloves, and the handbag.

Abbey was left to assume when she got upstairs she took a shower, washed his shoes inside and out, toweled herself dry, put her clothes back on, and left the frat house before anyone happened to show up.

What a stupid plan! Eighty guys live in that frat house! Yes, they were all scheduled to be at Thon, but the odds of every single guy being away during the murder and subsequent shower have to be astronomical!

And yet...it seems to have worked, since no one seems to know who killed Tommy.

Chapter 11

THE LAST THING ABBEY saw on the video: one of the frat guys brought a girl into the basement for what appeared to be consensual sex. But before things had a chance to heat up they saw Tommy's body and freaked. Suddenly there were eight or nine guys in the room, including Colson, all shouting, taking pictures on cell phones, moving around to get closer looks, totally contaminating the crime scene. Abbey could see Colson searching the room with his eyes. Moments later, he was staring directly into the camera...

And then it went dark.

Now she's at Dooley's, sitting at the bar with Cameron and two other sorority sisters, Maggie and Blair, and Cameron's telling Blair off because she made the mistake of saying she felt sorry for Tommy's parents. Cameron's lecturing her about how Tommy's parents tried to destroy Abbey's reputation, how they threatened to sue the college, and how much money they spent on attorneys to get the case thrown out...but Abbey isn't chiming in. She's too busy thinking about the MILF who killed Tommy. Wouldn't she have to be the mother of one of the girls Tommy raped?

Yes, absolutely.

Except that the MILF specifically asked Tommy if he remembered Hailey.

Over the past three semesters, Abbey and six others reported Tommy had raped them. But none of the six were named Hailey, which means if Tommy raped her, she didn't tell the school.

Just her mom.

Abbey interrupts Cameron's diatribe. "Do any of you know a girl named Hailey?"

They do, but only Maggie knows a student named Hailey. "Hailey something," she says. "Capshaw, I think. Something like that."

"Where's she from?"

Maggie shrugs. "Chattanooga?" She thinks a minute. "I'm not sure. We were on some committee last year, and she was great. This year she kind of shut down, turned anorexic."

"You sure she's not local?"

"I don't think so, but...want me to ask her?"

"You have her number?"

She points across the room. "Three tables over. The skinny chick? Ball cap, ponytail?"

"That's her?"

"What's left of her."

Abbey leans forward to get a better look, but the place is too crowded, so she stands up.

Cameron says, "What about her?"

Abbey sits down, but keeps staring.

"Abbey?" Cameron repeats.

"Yeah?"

"What's with this Hailey chick?"

"Someone asked if I knew her."

"Who?"

"It's not important."

"Colson Ford?"

Abbey looks at her. "No."

"You sure?"

"Positive. Let it go, Cam, okay?"

"Yeah, whatever."

Blair says, "Are you guys okay?"

Cameron says, "Not really. Colson threatened Abbey tonight at Thon. When she told him off he cussed her out and stomped off. Later, after they hauled Tommy out in the body bag, Abbey and Colson had a long, private talk, but Abbey won't tell me what he said."

Abbey frowns. "Thanks, Cam."

"My pleasure."

Naturally, Blair and Maggie start in on her like buzzards on a carcass: "What did he *say*?" "Did he *see* anything?" "Does he know who killed Tommy?"

"Jesus!" Abbey says. "Lighten up! He was just apologizing for being a jerk."

They look at Cameron, who says, "I couldn't hear the discussion, but I guarantee he wasn't apologizing."

Abbey says, "At first he was upset about Tommy. But eventually, he apologized for how they all treated me. He asked me to forgive him."

Cameron raises an eyebrow. "I hope you told him to fuck himself."

"I accepted his apology, but said we'd never be friends."

"Good for you!" Blair says.

"Guys?" Maggie says. "I've still got $19 left on my debit card. Who wants a drink?"

They all do.

Halfway into the round, Abbey gets a call from Dani Ripper, the private detective she and her parents hired six months ago to build a case against Tommy. Dani saw the news about Tommy on TV and assumed Abbey killed him. Now she's threatening to tell the police that Abbey asked about hiring a hitman.

Thanks, Dani!

Then she gives Abbey a long, drawn out lecture about why she shouldn't talk to the police without an attorney. Gives her a million reasons why she shouldn't. Even if she's innocent.

Whatever.

Abbey doesn't need advice. She's way ahead of the game.

She tells Dani what Dani wants to hear, then goes back to her celebration. It's a little weird laughing and toasting the death of a college student, regardless of the circumstances. But what Tommy did to her was far worse than rape. He and his parents held organized rallies and met with fraternities and athletes to plead their case and explain what could happen if girls like Abbey were allowed to topple the institutions they hold sacred, like football and fraternities. Not all, but hundreds of students took up the challenge to make Abbey's life a living hell.

Cameron's holding her glass up, offering a toast. Abbey and the others lift their glasses as Cameron says: "I have two words for our dearly departed Tommy Kern: *Fuck you, Tommy!*"

"That's three words," Blair says.

"Was it? I must be drunker than I thought."

"He's immortal," Abbey says.

Cam frowns. "What do you mean?"

"They're never gonna get all his blood out of that concrete floor."

"So?"

"As long as that house remains standing, people will remember Tommy Kern, and how he died there."

Cam says, "On the bright side, I bet no girl will ever go in *that* basement again!"

"I bet it'll be just the opposite. They won't be able to *keep* girls from going down there. It'll wind up being some sort of creepy shrine. I bet that fucking basement will get ten times the action after this."

Cam frowns. "People are so *weird!*"

Abbey's thinking, *you should know, Cam. You're weirder than most.*

Cam now saying, "Oh shit!"

Abbey looks up just in time to see an angry woman heading toward them at a fast clip. By the time she realizes it's Nancy Kern, it's too late. Nancy gives her a hard slap across the face.

Cameron jumps to her feet, grabs Nancy by the shoulders, and pushes her against the bar. Then she and Nancy start screaming at each other.

Suddenly, out of nowhere, four frat guys—Tommy's buddies—are restraining Cameron, which allows Nancy to turn her attention to Abbey and the others. She gives them a withering look and her voice explodes: "You're *celebrating?*"

There's a lot going on: the slap hurt like hell—*still* hurts like hell, and came out of nowhere. Abbey's fighting to keep from crying. Cam's cussing the frat boys, trying to kick and bite them, and is generally succeeding. Maggie and Blair are off their stools, wide-eyed and terrified. Nancy singles them out: "You think that's *appropriate?* My son is *dead!*"

With a face contorted into a ghoulish mask of sadness and fury, Nancy turns to Abbey, even as bar security can be heard making their way toward the action. At that point everyone—even Cam—goes quiet, waiting to hear what Abbey has to say.

And she doesn't disappoint.

She stares directly into Nancy's eyes and says, "Tommy was a sweet guy. Everybody loved him. We're celebrating his life, not his death."

Nancy says, "I'll just *bet* you are, you trashy little *slut!* But you're right about one thing: Tommy had lots of friends. She looks at the four frat guys, then back at Abbey. "I wouldn't want to be *you.* Not on *this* campus. Not after *this.*"

Abbey says, "*Really*, Mrs. Kern? Because with him in a body bag, I think my chances of *not* getting beaten or raped just went through the roof."

Nancy lunges at her across the table, and now three of the frat guys are trying to hold her back. The other one—Colson—appears to be suppressing a smile. At this point two things happen: first, security finally makes their way through the crowd and begins escorting Mrs. Kern and the boys out of the bar. Second, Abbey's phone rings. She checks the number, tells the caller, "Hold on a minute," then tells her friends, "I'm gonna find a quiet place. Keep the party going, I'll be right back."

There aren't many quiet places in Dooley's, but when she finally finds one Abbey puts the phone to her ear and says:

Chapter 12

"WHAT THE FUCK ARE YOU DOING?" "This is my actual cell phone number!"

Toby says, "I tried the other one several times, but you didn't answer."

"I told you never to call this number!"

"I know. But I was concerned."

"Why? What's wrong?"

"Tommy Kern was murdered tonight."

"That's a *good* thing. He *raped* me, remember? What's the problem?"

"The problem is you knew about Tommy *before* you gave me the box to hold."

"So?"

"I'm—I just want to know how big a favor I'm doing here."

"Are you having second thoughts?"

"No, but—"

"You want me to sweeten the pot? Is that it?"

"What do you mean?"

"You want something from me. Money? Sexual favors?"

"No, of *course* not! Just—some sort of reassurance that..."

"Are you asking if I killed him?"

"No. I mean, if you did, I don't want to know."

"I can't believe you think I'm capable of that. The answer's no. I didn't kill him. I was hosting an all-night dance-a-thon for our sorority when it happened. There are literally hundreds of people who can verify my exact whereabouts at the time of the crime. And before you ask, no, I didn't hire anyone to do it. This was a complete and total shock to me."

"So the box has nothing to do with Tommy?"

She goes quiet.

"Abbey?"

"I heard you, I'm just trying to figure out how to answer that. You and I have become really close, Toby, and I don't ever want to lie to you. I mean, I probably *would* have before tonight, but not now. Not after what you've done for me. I trust you more than anyone in the world right now, and I don't want to screw that up."

"Thank you."

"I can't give you details, but I *will* say this much, and hope you won't repeat it: I was working on a project that involved exposing other rapes, including Tommy's. It has nothing to do with killing him, but it's something I wouldn't want the police to find if they consider me a suspect. But again, it has nothing to do with me being guilty in any way. You have my word."

"It's okay, Abbey. I'd keep the box safe for you even if it contained murder evidence."

She holds the phone away from her ear and stares at it.

Can he possibly be *serious*?

She hopes so.

She returns the phone to her ear and says, "Thank you. You're an amazing friend."

"You're an amazing girl."

"Thank you, Toby." She takes a deep breath. "Not to ruin the mood, but what are we gonna do about this phone call?"

"What do you mean?"

"If the police know who killed Tommy, there's no problem. But if they're flying blind, they'll want to interview me."

"Like you said, you've got the perfect alibi."

"That doesn't mean they won't check my phone records. If they do, they'll find your number and wonder who you are and what we talked about. What'll you say if they ask you?"

"I'll tell them we're friends who met at a bar, and dated a couple of times."

"And why did you call me tonight?"

"I'll say our relationship never took off because of what Tommy did, and how it affected you. I'll tell them we haven't spoken in months, but tonight I was watching TV and saw he'd been murdered, and called to ask if you heard the news. No big deal."

"You can't tell them we dated."

"Why not?"

"This is the first and only phone call we've exchanged on this number. If you say we dated, the police will wonder why there are no phone records or text messages between us."

"Good point."

"If they talk to you, just tell them how we met, and that you knew all about Tommy from back then, and you called tonight to see if I heard the news. Will that work?"

"Yeah. I can do that."

"Good. That'll be our story. But...you can't call me again at this number, okay?"

"Okay."

"Also, whatever happens, don't turn your phone over to the police, because my throwaway phone number's on it, and they might be able to trace it to the store where I bought it. If they pull the video from the purchase—"

"I'm with you," he says. "Shit!"

"What's wrong?"

"None of this would be a problem if I hadn't called this number. I'm really sorry, Abbey."

"It's okay. Hopefully the police will figure out who killed him, and none of this will ever come up. But do me a favor?"

"Anything."

"Erase this call from your phone, and I'll do the same. It's not a perfect solution, but it's better than nothing."

"No problem. Do you back your phone up to the cloud?"

"No."

"Good. Don't start."

"Okay."

"Abbey?"

"Yeah?"

"I know I can't call this number again, but can you check your other phone twice a day, in case something happens and I need to get a hold of you?"

"Of course. And...thanks again for holding the box."

"Thanks for trusting me."

She hangs up. Erases the call from her phone log. Shakes her head, thinking, *Fuck! After all the planning I did to distance myself from Toby and the box, I can't believe he called this number! FUCK!*

The second *fuck* has nothing to do with Toby's phone call.

It's her reaction at seeing Hailey Capshaw entering the lady's room just now...

With Cameron Reeder.

Chapter 13

ABBEY WAITS AT A distance till Hailey leaves. Then she enters the lady's room to find Cameron standing in front of the mirror.

"I thought you didn't know her."

"I didn't," Cameron says. "But after what happened tonight, I wanted to."

"Why?"

"I could tell you weren't being honest with me about this whole Colson thing. I think you guys know a lot more than you're saying."

"Like what?"

"Like Colson and Hailey were involved in Tommy's murder."

"That's crazy."

"Is it? First, right out of the blue, you ask if we know a chick named Hailey."

Abbey says, "Is there a second thing, or is that it?"

"I saw the smirk Colson gave you when you stood up to Mrs. Kern."

"Let's recap. You've come to the conclusion Colson and Hailey murdered Tommy because I asked if you knew a girl named Hailey and Colson smirked at me."

"Deny it all you want."

"Thanks. I will."

Cam shoots her a look. "Does that mean you don't want to hear what Hailey told me just now?"

Chapter 14

"YOU AND HAILEY SPOKE?"

"We did."

"How did that come about?"

"I went to her table, introduced myself, and asked if I could talk to her in private."

"And she followed you to the *bathroom?* Just like that?"

"Yup. I mean, she asked what it was about, and I asked if she saw the big scene with Mrs. Kern and the frat guys.' She said 'Of course,' and I told her we were out in front of the frat house earlier tonight, watching them haul Tommy off in the body bag, and one of the frat guys asked if we knew a girl named Hailey. Naturally, she wanted to know which guy said that, and I told her to follow me to the lady's room."

"So what happened?"

"I'll skip the small talk and get to the part we care about: she said she knew who Tommy Kern was, but she'd never met him."

"And you believed her?"

"Totally. But when she asked which frat guy asked about her, I said 'Colson Ford,' and her face turned white. I mean she nearly collapsed right there on the floor."

"You might be imagining that part."

"No way. She definitely knows Colson. She was scared shitless. I think she killed Tommy, and Colson found out."

Abbey sighs. "Once again, you've allowed your imagination to run wild. You just finished telling me she never met Tommy."

"So?"

"So why would she stab him to death?"

"I don't know. Maybe he dragged her down there and tried to rape her and didn't know she had a knife."

"She was in the bar with friends."

"So?"

"Don't you think she seemed awfully cool for a girl who supposedly stabbed a guy 27 times less than two hours earlier? And again, you said they never met. How could she possibly say that convincingly if he dragged her down to the basement to rape her?"

"I don't know. But *something's* going on. And you and Colson know more than you're letting on."

"Colson doesn't know shit."

"Look me in the eye and tell me he's not the one who asked you about Hailey."

She looks Cam in the eye. "Colson didn't ask me about Hailey."

Cam says, "Then who did?"

"Tommy."

"What? Bullshit! You didn't talk to Tommy tonight."

"I never said it happened tonight. I saw him a couple of weeks ago. He asked me if I knew her."

"Why?"

"I don't know. But I remembered it tonight when we were talking about him."

"That might be proof."

"Of what?"

"If he was asking about her, then maybe he—"

"Cam?"

"Yeah?"

"Give it up, okay?"

"Why?"

"Because whoever killed him did every girl on this campus a favor. And there's no way Hailey could possibly kill Tommy. He outweighs her by a hundred and fifty pounds!"

"You think Colson did it?"

"I don't know. But if he did, I hope he gets away with it."

"You know what I think?"

"What now?"

"I think Colson killed Tommy, and Hailey saw him leaving the frat house right afterward."

"If that's true he would've been covered in blood."

"Exactly."

Abbey rolls her eyes. "Let it go, Cam."

"Sorry. I hate that bastard."

Abbey's phone rings. She looks at the caller ID and says, "Speak of the devil. It's Colson."

"Put him on speaker. I dare you."

She does. Colson says, "Abbey? Don't leave the bar alone tonight."

"Why not?"

"The guys have been drinking. I think they're planning to jump you."

Her lip starts quivering. "Thanks, Colson."

He says, "You shouldn't have done that tonight. The whole celebration thing? Everyone's talking about it. Plus, what you said to Mrs. Kern? The guys are really pissed. You're not safe."

"I know. I'm sorry."

"Am I on speaker?"

"No. I'm in the lady's room. It's the echo."

"You can't tell anyone I warned you."

"I won't."

"Be careful, okay?"

"I will. I've got it covered."

"You sure? Because if something goes down, I won't be able to help you."

"I know. Thanks again."

When she hangs up Cam says, "Okay. I believe you."

"About what?"

"He's trying to be your friend."

"You finally realize that?"

"Yes. My only question is...*why?*"

"*Jesus!*" Abbey says, in total frustration. "Will you *ever* let this go?"

"No. But we can talk about it later. What's your plan for getting home safely?"

"I'm calling the cops."

"Now?"

"Uh huh. Want to listen in?"

"Of course."

Abbey calls the police and says, "My life's in danger." She tells them how Tommy's mother assaulted her and threatened her safety. They switch her to a Lieutenant Palmer, who says he's pleased to hear from her, since he was just about to send a detective to her sorority.

"Why?"

"We'd like to ask you a few questions about Tommy Kern."

"How many?"

"Excuse me?"

"Exactly how many questions would you like to ask?"

He pauses. "That depends on your answers."

"You'll ask if I killed Tommy and I'll say no. You'll ask if I knew who did and I'll say no. You'll ask where I was at the time of his death and I'll tell you. What else could you possibly need to know?"

"There might be a couple more questions. But it shouldn't take too long."

"I've seen *Dateline*. I don't want to be stuck in an interrogation room for 10 hours."

"We don't do that."

"When do you want to talk?"

"As soon as possible."

"Am I a suspect?"

"We're just gathering some background."

"Does that mean I'm a suspect?"

"Should you be?"

"Am I?"

He says, "Are you willing to talk to me about Tommy Kern?"

"Yes."

"When can you come in?"

"Now."

"You want me to send someone to pick you up?"

"That depends. I'm at Dooley's Bar, and there's a million people here."

"So?"

"I don't want them to see me getting into a cop car. Do you have unmarked cars?"

"I can probably get one."

"And a cop who's not in uniform?"

"That might be a problem."

"In that case, don't worry about it. I'll get my own ride."

She hangs up.

Cam says, "Want me to call Uber?"

"Yes. Thanks."

"Can I come with you?"

She laughs. "No fucking way! If you tell them your smirk theory, they'll put us both in jail!"

Five hours later Lieutenant Palmer leaves Abbey alone in the interrogation room for the third time. When he comes back he says, "What can you tell me about Colson Ford?"

She shrugs. "What do you want to know?"

"Whatever you feel like sharing."

"Well, I don't know him that well. I mean, he's one of Tommy's fraternity brothers, and one of the ringleaders of the group of guys who always bullied me."

"When's the last time you saw him?"

"Tonight." She looks at her watch. "I mean, last night. At the bar."

"At Dooley's?"

"Uh huh. He was one of the four guys who was there with Tommy's mother."

"And he left with Mrs. Kern and the others?"

"Yes."

"And that's the last time you heard from him?"

She pauses. Something in the way he asked that question makes her look at him. It's like he was trying too hard to sound casual. And suddenly all the warnings Dani Ripper gave her about talking to the police are flooding her brain. Every ounce of intuition she possesses is screaming this one, indisputable fact:

Lieutenant Palmer knows Colson called her cell phone.

But why should that matter?

"Abbey?"

"He called me last night. Moments before I called you."

"He called your cell phone?"

She nods.

"Is that why you refused to let us look at your phone?"

"You didn't ask to look at it, you asked if I'd turn it over to you."

"And you refused."

"Just to be clear, I didn't refuse to surrender my phone to you. I said if you insist on *taking* it, I'd have to hire an attorney and ask his opinion. And when I said that, you practically shit your pants and told me not to worry about the phone."

Lieutenant Palmer stares at her a long moment, then says, "I stand corrected." He leans back in his chair and says, "Had Colson ever called you before last night?"

"Many times. They all did."

"You're referring to the group that threatened and bullied you?"

She looks down. "Yes."

"And is that why he called you last night? To threaten you?"

"No. He called to warn me."

Lieutenant Palmer perks up. "About what?"

"He said a bunch of Tommy's friends had gotten all worked up because my friends and I were celebrating Tommy's death. Colson said the guys were planning to jump me."

"And you believed him?"

"Yes."

"What does that mean to you?"

"Sir?"

"He said they were planning to *jump* you. What did you take that to mean?"

"It means they were going to beat the shit out of me, and possibly gang rape me."

"Here's what I don't understand: you said Colson was one of the ringleaders, correct?"

She nods.

"So why would he call to warn you?"

"The first time I saw Colson last night was at the dance. He and a bunch of the guys paid to get on my dance card so they could insult and intimidate me all night. He said some ugly things, I yelled at him, and he left the dance."

"Did he say where he was going?"

"No."

"You're sure?"

"I only remember the threats he made and the names he called me. But later on, he was standing near me when the police took Tommy's body to the ambulance and asked if he could talk to me. I said yes, and he apologized for the way he treated me. Not just at the dance, but the last six months."

"Did he say why the sudden change of heart?"

"Tommy's death shook him."

"Is it possible he thought you killed Tommy and he might be next on your list?"

"He knows I didn't kill Tommy. I was at the dance."

"Maybe so, but he didn't necessarily know *when* Tommy was killed, correct?"

Abbey shrugs. "I'm not sure what he knew, or when."

"Could Colson have killed Tommy?"

"You mean after he left the dance?"

"Yes. Or possibly before he showed up at the dance."

"I have no idea. Maybe you should ask Colson. You want his number?"

"Do you have it?"

"Of course. I just told you he called me last night."

She removes her phone from her jeans pocket and turns it on. After a moment she says, "Got a pen?"

Lieutenant Parker says, "Could you call him for me?"

"Why?"

"I'd like to see your reaction."

"To what?"

"To the detective's voice telling you Colson Ford is dead."

Chapter 15

"COLSON'S DEAD?"

"You don't sound too broken up about it."

"Why should I be?"

"According to you, he called to warn you about an impending assault."

"Or maybe he was setting me up for something worse."

"You don't sound very trusting."

"I used to trust people a lot more before I got raped. Even after that, I trusted my college. But when I asked for help, they threatened legal action, took my scholarship, and painted me as a liar. I used to trust policemen—and detectives, and even lieutenants—but like Dani Ripper said, you're all a bunch of liars."

He sits up straighter. "Dani Ripper said that?"

"Yup. And she's right."

"How so?"

"When I turned on my phone just now, there were three messages from Colson asking if I was okay. The most recent message was ten minutes ago."

There's zero mirth behind Lieutenant Palmer's flat smile as he says, "For the record, I never said Colson Ford was dead. I said I wanted to see your reaction to *hearing* he was dead. And I *did* see it."

"Fine. Are you arresting me?"

"Should I?"

"No. Are you?"

"Not at this time."

"Then I'm free to go?"

"For now? Sure. But rest assured, we're going to check out everything you told us."

"I'd expect no less."

Abbey stands, starts to leave.

Lieutenant Palmer says, "Give my regards to Ms. Ripper."

Abbey says, "While we're on the subject, I should probably tell you something: Dani's going to contact you about something I said, months ago."

"Just so you know, I don't put much stock in anything Dani Ripper says."

"Good. Because I asked if she knew any hitmen I could hire to kill Tommy Kern."

Palmer's eyes bug out. His face turns two shades of blue. He chokes, jumps to his feet; then hunches over, hands-on-knees, and coughs violently. Then he straightens his body, lurches, grabs the table for support. Finally he clears his throat loudly, points to the empty chair, and says, "Sit your ass down."

Chapter 16

THE HITMAN REVELATION SOUNDED worse than it was. It didn't take Lieutenant Palmer long to dismiss the idea, and in fact, 24 hours after she walked into the police station, he publicly announced Abbey had cooperated fully and was no longer a suspect in Tommy's murder. The police went one step further and asked Abbey to make a list of the frat boys who'd been harassing her. Since there were too many to name, she wrote down the worst offenders and the police met and threatened each of them with jail time if they bothered her again. As a result, Abbey felt safer at school than she had since her pre-rape days. Beyond that, she was virtually ignored by the police. Had she not been so paranoid, she would have begun searching for Tommy's killer immediately.

But she *was* paranoid, and has remained so because like she said, she's not Sonny Wortzik. So she waited an entire week, just in case. It was torture, sitting around, doing nothing. But eventually she felt safe enough to begin the process. Where to start?

The Online Student Directory, of course.

It would be so simple to open her laptop and search the various spellings for coeds named Hailey, then try to locate Facebook photos for their moms. But if Abbey learned anything from Dani Ripper, it's that cops can't be trusted. Yes, she took a polygraph, and let them copy the data from her "every day" laptop and yes, she finally relented and gave them her cell phone for what was supposed to be sixty minutes, but turned out to be two-plus hours, and yes they interviewed a half-dozen kids who saw her at the dance. But still, it didn't make sense for the detectives to rule her out so quickly. So even though Abbey's optimistic, she remains on high alert and assumes the police are keeping an eye on her, hoping she'll grow complacent enough to make a mistake. She's fully aware they could show up at any moment to ask more questions, search her car, her room and personal belongings, and check her recent phone and computer records.

With this in mind, Abbey considers her options:

1. She could go to the library (local, not the college one) and use a public computer. But if the police *are* following her, it would be a simple matter for them to cordon off the computer she used and pull her search records from it.

2. She could ask to borrow a sorority sister's computer. But that would certainly create suspicion, and could possibly lead to an "anonymous" call to the police.

3. She could retrieve the box that contains her secret laptop. But again, if the police are following her, they'll

probably see the exchange being made. And if not, just *possessing* her secret laptop could put her in prison, since it contains not only the rape videos, but also the live murder video and all her extortion information. If *anyone* gets their hands on that laptop—whether civilian or cop—she's toast. Not to mention the envelopes, the $350,000 in cash...and the fake ID's she hasn't used yet.

Abbey's fourth option is the only viable one. She retrieves her throwaway phone and calls Toby. When he answers she says, "I got your message of congratulations. That was sweet."

"I knew you didn't do it," he says.

"Really?" she teases. "I seem to remember you being pretty damn worried last week."

"Well..."

"It's okay. Can I ask you something?"

"Of course."

"How many favors do I have left in our friendship quiver?"

"How many do you need?"

"Can you run a search for me?"

"Of course."

"Thanks! You're the best."

Abbey tells him what she needs and he agrees to text her the results as soon as he gets them. An hour later Toby sends her a text message that includes five names, five Facebook addresses, and five photos. The names are the various Haileys currently enrolled at the college. The Facebook addresses belong to their mothers. The photos are the ones associated with the home page of each Facebook account.

Abbey goes straight to the photos and finds three moms and two photos of children. The moms look nothing like the MILF who killed Tommy. Moments later, the two "missing" moms appear. Toby explained he pulled them from their Facebook photo galleries.

But neither of these women killed Tommy.

Shit!

Abbey clenches her teeth in frustration. She was so certain she'd gotten it right. When the MILF said "Remember Hailey?" before killing Tommy, Abbey assumed:

1. The MILF had a daughter named Hailey
2. Tommy Kern raped her
3. This was the mom's motive for killing him

It seemed so incredibly obvious and logical at the time!

But now that her theory's been proven wrong, Abbey's forced to admit her conclusions were clearly influenced by her personal experience. Knowing there must be a dozen other possibilities she failed to consider, she starts naming them in her mind: the MILF might be a serial killer who happened to meet Tommy that night. She might not have a daughter at all. Hailey could be her sister. She...

Abbey's phone pings with another set of names and photos, and she has to laugh. Talk about making assumptions! Hailey's a popular name for Abbey's age group. What made her assume there were only five coeds in the whole college named Hailey?

This set contains two additional Haileys, but...neither of the mom's faces and bodies are remotely similar to the mom who killed Tommy.

Abbey sighs.

Is it worth a shot to click on each Facebook link to view the entire collection of photos?

Probably not. Surely Toby wouldn't send any photo he hadn't verified. She waits a few minutes, then calls him back.

"Was that everyone?" she asks.

"Every Hailey," he says.

"And you're sure you sent me the right moms?"

"That's what took so long." He waits for her to say something. When she doesn't, he offers, "If you'll tell me what you're trying to achieve I'm sure I could help you."

"I know. But..."

"You can't?"

"No. Sorry."

"That's okay. Is there anything else you need?"

"No, but I *would* like to pay you for your time."

"No need. It was just an hour, and we're friends."

She laughs. "I could have made it easier for you."

"How?"

"I could have told you to ignore the Raggedy Anns."

"What do you mean?"

"I should have mentioned the mom I'm looking for is one of the hottest older women I've ever seen. A total MILF."

"Well, if she's hotter than that last one, she must be *amazing*."

"You thought the last one was *hot?*"

"Uh, hello...didn't *you?*"

Abbey laughs. "Are you *serious?* She was the worst of the bunch!"

He laughs. "Well, she's better than I'll ever get."

"Don't be so hard on yourself, Toby. I swear, if you don't gain some confidence I'm gonna change your name to Eeyore. I *guarantee* you can do better. And if you'd like, I'll help you find someone special."

"Can you get me *that* one?"

Abbey laughs again. "Stop it. You're gonna make me pee my pants."

They hang up and she laughs again, just thinking about it. Hard to believe he could possibly find that bow wow attractive. Proves there's someone for everyone.

She makes a peanut butter sandwich and tries to think of other reasons why the MILF asked Tommy if he remembered Hailey. But her mind keeps going back to her recent conversation. What could Toby possibly see in that photo that turned him on?

Must be the boobs.

Abbey was so busy studying the faces she probably overlooked the boobs. She grabs her phone, checks the most recent photo and finds...

Chapter 17

THE WOMAN IS EVEN uglier than Abbey remembered.

But she *does* have gigantic boobs.

Well, to each his own, Abbey thinks as she studies the photo in detail, and comes to the conclusion she'll never understand men. It would be one thing if this lady's tits were shapely, or well-proportioned, but no: they're enormous, droopy, and would probably sag to the poor woman's ankles, if not for the ample belly fat holding them in check.

Abbey considers calling Toby back to tease him about it, but before she can, her phone pings with a message that says:

> *This bounced back to me, so I'm resending*
> *in case you didn't get it the first time.*

You know those moments that change your life?
This is one of those.

Abbey opens the file to see the gorgeous face and body of Tommy's killer. She scrolls down to see the name...Lauren Capshaw...and knows her world will never be the same.

And now she's on the phone again, telling Toby she needs the box back, ASAP.

"I'm at work," he says.

"Can you get away?"

"Let me check."

The phone goes silent for a moment. When he comes back on the line the news is good: "I'm available," he says.

"Great! But we need to be careful."

"Of course. You got a plan?"

"I do."

She tells him, and he says he'll need an hour.

Chapter 18

ABBEY'S PLAN IS SIMPLE: she'll sit tight for 30 minutes, then drive around the city till Toby has time to get to the mall and park near the front entrance. Then she'll drive there and look for his car. When she sees it, she'll find a parking space, and he'll watch the front entrance for cops as Abbey enters the mall and walks immediately to the far end. If the coast is clear, he'll drive around the mall and pick her up outside the back entrance of Verite Beauty. If he's not there when she walks out, it means he saw something suspicious, and had to abort the plan. If he *is* there, she'll get in his car and he'll drive her to the Hampton Inn, where he'll get her a room in his name, so she can work on her project in private. She figures if the police are following her, they'll keep an eye on her car and wait for her to return. By the time she does, her video will be edited, and Toby will once again have the box.

It's a perfect plan, and everything goes perfectly until it doesn't.

Toby picked Abbey up behind Verite, no problem. Drove her to the hotel, got the room while she waited in the car. Then he went back to his car, gave her the room key, pulled a suitcase out of the trunk, gave it to her, watched her roll it behind her into the lobby. Then saw two men escorting her back out of the lobby. He tried to back out of his parking space and get away, but found his car blocked by a navy sedan.

Now, one of the men introduces himself as a detective, and tells him to get out of his car. When he does, they pat him down and ask his permission to search his car. He lets them. While one detective leans Abbey against his car and pats her down the other asks for Toby's driver's license and registration, runs a check on him, and asks how he and Abbey know each other. Then one of the detectives looks at Abbey and says, "It's one-sixteen. Reason I'm telling you this, it's your moment of truth. What's in the suitcase?"

Toby says, "She wants a lawyer."

The detective says, "Is that true?"

And Abbey says, "Before I answer, let me ask *you* a question. What do *you* think is in it?"

"Judging from all the evasive maneuvers you made to get here, I'd say it's evidence in a murder case."

"And if it is?"

"Then you're both in big trouble."

"Okay," Abbey says.

"Okay what?"

"I'll tell you why we went to so much trouble just now."
She pauses, then says, "Toby and I were going to have sex in this hotel."

The detective looks at Abbey, then Toby, then back at Abbey. "You and this guy."

"That's right."

"I don't believe it."

Abbey shrugs.

The other detective says, "If that's true, why didn't he just pick you up at the sorority house and bring you here?"

"He's got a girlfriend."

"*This* guy does. The one you call Toby."

"That's right."

"And why do you call him that?"

"You know the show, *The Office?*"

"What about it?"

"He identifies with the character Toby Flenderson."

First detective looks at him. "Your girlfriend: is this a real girl, or a blow up doll?"

"Real."

"Where do you work, son?"

"Dani Ripper Detective Agency."

"You—Oh *shit!*"

Other detective says, "What's wrong?"

"He's Dani Ripper's computer nerd."

"I'm Dani's *partner*," Dillon corrects.

"Right. Whatever. And you've got a girlfriend?"

"Yes. A very jealous one."

"Please tell me it's Dani Ripper!"

"It's not."

The detective laughs. "You thought I was *serious?*"

Dillon shrugs.

"So you're cheating on your jealous girlfriend with this young lady, Miss Rayne."

"Why *wouldn't* I? I mean, *look* at her!"

He does, and Abbey tries to blush.

The detective frowns. "No offense, son, but she's *way* out of your league. Are you blackmailing her?"

"Of course not."

"Supplying her with illegal drugs?"

"No."

"If that's true, the only reason I can think a girl like this would agree to have sex with a guy like you is if you've been holding murder evidence for her. Is that what's in this suitcase?"

"No."

Addressing Abbey, the first detective says, "He gave you the suitcase, then got back in the car, and you walked into the lobby alone."

"So?"

"If he came here for sex, why get back in the car after giving you the suitcase?"

"He was waiting for me to get dressed up."

"You mean undressed, don't you?"

"No. He brought me a sexy outfit he wanted me to wear for the occasion."

"What occasion?"

"It's our first time."

"Have you seen it yet? The outfit?"

"No. It was supposed to be a surprise."

The detective looks skeptical. "Let me see if I've got this straight: you expect us to believe this guy Dillon has an actual girlfriend. Not only that, but he somehow got *you* to agree to have sex with him. And he picked out a sexy outfit for you to wear, and he put it in this very suitcase."

"Correct."

"And if we hadn't stopped you in the lobby just now, you would have gone to the room and put on the outfit and a few minutes later he would have joined you?"

"That's right."

The detectives look at each other and burst into laughter. Then one says, "If everything you said is true, I can't imagine why you'd object to showing us the outfit and anything else he might have put in the suitcase."

"You really can't imagine why I'd object to that?"

"No."

"How about because it's personal, private, and terribly embarrassing?"

"So's a jail sentence."

Abbey looks at the suitcase, then at Dillon. "Fine," she says. "Open it."

"No!" Dillon says.

The detective looks at him. "Who's suitcase is it?"

"Mine."

"And you're refusing to let us open it?"

He looks at Abbey.

She says, "It'll be okay."

Dillon sighs.

The detective says, "May I?"

Dillon shrugs, and the detective opens the suitcase.

Chapter 19

THE MOST IMPORTANT FEATURE of Abbey's plan was that this would be a dry run. If everything went smoothly, she'd walk into Dillon's hotel room with the suitcase and he'd drive home, pick up the actual box, and bring it to her. She told him to buy a sexy outfit and put it in the suitcase, just in case the police followed them. Dillon asked if the sexy outfit was really necessary, and she assured him it was vital.

"I'll reimburse you," she said, and he told her he'd need an hour to get his suitcase, buy a sexy outfit, and drive to the mall.

Now, as the detectives stare at the "sexy" outfit, they're stunned into silence. There are two articles of clothing: a bra and panties.

If you can call them that.

Abbey no longer needs to pretend she's blushing, her face is genuinely crimson, and she's glaring at Dillon.

After making sure there's nothing else in the suitcase, the first detective holds up the enormous, dated, industrial-strength bra, then the gigantic pair of plastic granny panties. Then both detectives look at Abbey's face and laugh their asses off.

After they leave, Dillon follows Abbey into the hotel room and remains standing as she sits in the chair and puts her face in her hands. He tries to apologize, but she waves off his words and walks to the bathroom and washes her face with cold water, trying to get her cheeks back to normal.

But they remain bright red.

She takes a deep breath, exits the bathroom and says, "That's the most humiliating thing that ever happened to me. And I'm including the four-hour rape kit."

"I'm sorry, Abbey. I—"

"You know the entire Nashville Police Department will be talking about this, right?"

"At least they don't think you killed that kid."

"I almost rather they did! I've been trying like hell to keep a low profile. You think this helps?"

"No. I'm really sorry. I—"

"Where the fuck did you get that monstrous bra and panties?"

"They're my grandmother's."

Abbey's jaw drops. "You live with your *grandmother?*"

"No."

"Well, she's obviously incontinent."

"No she's not. She's in heaven."

If Abbey were just a little less angry she would've thought, *Aww, how sweet.* Instead, she says, "What I meant was, did she used to pee herself?"

Dillon's look says she's crossed a line: "How should *I* know? Why would you ask *that?*"

"The rubber panties? Or whatever they are?"

"I just grabbed two things from the box."

"Which box is that?" Abbey asks, wondering if all the women in Dillon's life ask him to hold boxes for them.

"When granny was in hospice I boxed up her stuff. When I moved here I brought it with me and put it in my basement."

"Why?"

"I just never got around to donating it to Good Will."

"Lucky me."

He looks down at his feet. "I thought your plan was foolproof. I didn't expect the police to follow you."

Abbey says nothing so he adds, "Do you have any idea how embarrassing it would have been for me to walk into Victoria Secret and buy something sexy?"

She stares at him a moment, then holds her arms out and says, "Come here." She gives him a hug and says, "I'm sorry about your grandma. I can tell you really loved her. I wish someone loved me like that."

"Someone already does," he says.

She shows him a sad smile. "You might be the best person I know."

"A lot of good *that's* gonna do me."

"Don't pout, Toby."

"Can you call me Dillon?"

"Really?"

He nods.

"Okay. Dillon?"

"Yeah?"

"We need a plan."

He says, "The last one was perfect. I mean, how could the cops possibly know you came out the back entrance?"

Abbey looks at him. "You really don't know?"

He shakes his head.

"The phone call you made to me the night Tommy died."

"What about it?"

"The detectives were following *you* today, not me."

"*What?*"

"They must have found your deleted phone call on my cell phone."

"They're following *me?*"

"Yup."

"*Shit!* What should I *do?*"

"Donate your grandmother's clothes to Good Will."

"I'm being *serious*, Abbey!"

"Me too, Dillon. And while you're loading up her clothes, figure out a safe place to hide my box."

"It's already in a safe place."

"Is it at your house?"

He nods.

"Then it's not safe. They're probably asking a judge for a search warrant right now."

Dillon's hands are shaking. "We should call Dani."

"No fucking way!" She puts her hand on his shoulder and says, "Dillon? Look at me."

He does.

She says, "Do *not* call Dani."

"She'll know what to do. You can trust her."

"I can trust her to turn the box over to the police, you mean. Did you know she actually went to the police station to tell them I tried to hire a hitman?"

"Yeah. But she felt that was her duty."

"Exactly. And if she finds out *you're* involved, her duty will be to protect *you*."

"I think you're selling her short."

"Dillon, listen to me. You're Dani's partner. She can't afford to let you get caught withholding evidence in a murder investigation. She will fucking throw me under the bus to protect you and the business. And honestly? I can't blame her. So let's not put her in that position."

He sighs.

She says, "*Now* what's wrong?"

"You just said the box was evidence. Last week you said it wasn't."

Abbey takes a deep breath, lets it out slowly. When she speaks, her voice is tinged with annoyance: "I said the box is a project I was working on, and that's the truth. I also said I didn't kill Tommy, and that's the truth. But if the police get their hands on that box, they might jump to all the wrong conclusions. Instead of doing their job properly, they might decide to go after me."

"Why?"

"Because I'm the easy suspect, and the contents of the box will show I was working on something that involved the frat house rapes. They might think I was planning to get revenge, or plotting his murder, or whatever. But I wasn't. His death was a complete shock to me, and that's the truth."

Dillon sets his jaw. "Okay, we won't tell Dani. But what *should* we do?"

"Drive me to your place."

That surprises him. "Why on earth would you want to—?"

"I want to see what other clothes your granny has in your basement."

"*What?*"

She rolls her eyes. "That was a joke, Dillon."

"Oh."

She says, "I don't know if the police plan to search your home, but you were nice enough to help me, and I can't let you get in trouble. So if we get there first, you can give me the box, and I'll find another place to keep it. That way, you'll be safe."

"And if the police beat us there and start searching the place?"

"If they find it, I'll tell them I hid it in your home the night you brought me there to watch a movie."

"That never happened."

"Maybe not, but *they* don't know that. We'll say this happened Thursday night, two weeks ago, around 9 p.m. If they find the box they'll separate us and ask questions. You'll be able to honestly say you have no idea what's in the box, and I'll be able to tell them every last detail. After a couple of hours they'll have no choice but to let you go."

"Will you be able to find a safe place to keep it?"

She smiles. "I've already got a perfect place in mind."

Chapter 20

WHEN THEY GET TO Dillon's house, one of the detectives is waiting for them.

"Don't let him enter without a search warrant," Abbey whispers. "And if he has one, stay cool. Maybe he won't find it. And if he *does*, just act like you have no idea what it is."

"Okay."

"By the way, where is it?"

"Under my fish tank."

"Your *fish* tank?"

He smiles. "The base is almost a foot tall, but it looks like a solid piece of wood. They'd have to lift the tank off the table to look under it."

"I like it. Good job."

He grins.

She says, "I'd be able to lift it, right?"

"No way! It's super heavy. Why do you ask?"

"I'm supposed to have hidden it without your knowledge."

"Oh. Right."

"Don't worry. They probably won't find it."

He says, "You didn't need to lift it. You pulled the left end toward you and slid it off the table enough to fit the box under it. Then slid it back in place."

"Is that how you did it?"

"Yeah."

"Cool."

As it turns out, the detective doesn't have a search warrant. But he says his partner's working on it and should have it within the hour. He says, "You wouldn't believe how hard it was to get this warrant. We've been working on it all week. Your little trip to the mall really helped us out."

"Great," Dillon says.

The detective adds, "I'm not the jerk you think I am. I wasn't going to call you until my partner had the search warrant in his hand." He looks at Abbey and winks. "That way you lovebirds would have had at least an hour at the hotel to enjoy your sexy outfit."

He says, "But since I barely beat you here, either my partner and I killed the mood, or Toby got so excited all he managed to give you was a special *moment*."

Noting the forlorn look on Dillon's face, Abbey says, "I'd rather have one incredible minute with Dillon than an hour with anyone else."

"He's that much a stud, huh?"

"I can't speak for his girlfriend, but he certainly put a smile on *my* face."

The detective frowns. "You are so full of shit I bet turds pop out when you cough."

"That's a charming thing to say. I'm sure your wife would be so proud."

The detective was wrong about the search warrant. It took his partner two full hours to secure it. Then Dillon and Abbey had to wait another 30 minutes for the other cops to show up. They started the full-scale search by seizing Dillon's computer. For some reason that possibility hadn't occurred to him. Seeing the look of horror on his face, Abbey got him off to the side of the room and whispered, "What's wrong?"

He shakes his head.

"Are they gonna find some serious porn?"

"Worse. I'm fucked. I'm going to jail."

Her eyes go big. "Don't tell me you pulled a Jared!"

"What do you mean?"

"*Subway* Jared? *Underage* porn?"

His face registers shock. "No! It's..." he sighs. "Never mind." Moments later he says, "To make matters worse, I didn't enter "Quit" from the Ingame Menu."

"I'm sorry. Are you talking Geekspeak?"

He nods.

"What you're saying sounds serious, but I heard the word 'game' and can't help but think it's not as bad as you're making it sound. Can you translate?"

"I was playing *Resident Evil* this morning, and just as the Faceless Lady started attacking me with chainsaws, Dani called to say I was late for work. You have to get past her before you can press "save.""

"Have to get past Dani? Or the Faceless Lady?"

"The Faceless Lady. So anyway before I even started the game I took the precaution of creating a hack that would allow me to freeze the frame so I could pick up where I left off. And it worked! But now they've..."

He looks about to cry.

"They've what?"

"Unplugged my computer."

"And how does that affect whatever we're talking about?"

"It caused me to lose the connection."

"And this is like some sort of *Geek* Tragedy?"

He frowns. "It took me like five hours to get to that chapter of the game."

"You mean level?"

"No. This game has chapters, not levels."

Abbey stifles a laugh. "No offense, Dillon, but I'm pretty sure you'll be able to carve another five hours from your schedule."

"You don't understand. It's *Resident Evil 4*!"

"You're right. I *don't* understand."

"It's an old version of the game. I downloaded it." He looks around to make sure they're not being overheard. Then whispers, "*Illegally!*"

"*This* is what you're worried about? You illegally downloaded an old *video* game?"

Two hours later, as the first detective gathers the cops to conclude the search, he says, "Sorry about the mess. We tried to be as respectful as possible."

Dillon says, "When can I get my computer back?"

The detective says, "I don't know." He looks at his partner. "Weeks?"

The partner says, "Could be months."

Abbey says, "I was a murder suspect, and you guys only copied my files. Why can't you just copy his?"

"He's a well-known hacker. No telling *what's* on here."

Dillon closes his eyes, lifts his knees to his chest, starts rocking back and forth on the couch.

Abbey says, "That computer is his world. Any way to speed things up?"

The detective says, "I doubt it. On the bright side, it'll give him time to do something else."

"Like what?" Dillon says.

"Like hang out with your girlfriends, or play with your fish, or..." the detective looks at the cops and says, "Did you guys think to look under that fish tank?"

Chapter 21

DILLON'S TRYING TO LOOK COOL but he's coming across like Matthew McConaughey in the Lincoln commercials.

Not that Abbey's doing much better.

Her face has turned white and she's holding her hands to keep them from shaking.

She watches as two policemen lift the fish tank a foot above the table to find...

Nothing.

What?

Abbey shoots Dillon a curious look, but he doesn't see it. He's still rocking back and forth on the couch with his eyes closed, except that now he's hyperventilating.

The detective says, "Toby, you're breaking my heart. I'll see if I can get them to put a rush on your computer."

Dillon says nothing. It hasn't hit him yet.

When they leave, Abbey says, "What happened?"

"What do you mean?"

"Where's the box?"

"They didn't *find* it?"

"No."

"How could they possibly miss it?"

"It wasn't *there*, Dillon. You obviously moved it."

He jumps to his feet, slides one end of the tank toward him, reaches under it.

"You're wasting your time. The cops lifted the tank a whole foot off the table. The box isn't there."

"It *has* to be!"

"But it's not. *Think*, Dillon. Where else could you have put it?"

"No place. This is the only hiding place I've ever used."

"Do you have a roommate I don't know about?"

"No."

"What about your girlfriend?"

He frowns. "I don't have a girlfriend."

"I mean, have you had any girls over to spend the night?"

"Seriously, Abbey?"

"Dillon, I'm not going to coddle you about this. I fucking *trusted* you! If you swear this is the only place you could've put the box, I'm...I mean..."

She starts to cry.

Dillon rushes over, tries to console her.

"You have no idea!" she says, between sobs. "You think your fucking *game* download is serious? My life is *over*! I can't believe you *did* this to me!"

He says, "At least the police don't have it."

It takes her ten minutes to calm down enough to ask, "Who else knows about your hiding place?"

"No one."

"That's obviously not true. *Think!*"

"Well, I mean...just.."

She looks up at him. "Just who?"

"Dani. But she—"

"Dani Fucking RIPPER?"

"Yeah. But...she wouldn't—"

"Call her!"

"Huh?"

"Call the bitch! *Ask* her!"

"Dani's my partner and friend. She's not a bitch."

"If she stole my box..."

"She didn't."

"Fine. Call her."

"And say what?"

"Ask if she broke into your house and stole my box."

"She would never break into my house."

"How can you be so sure?"

"Because she's got a key."

Abbey puts her head in her hands and says, "Omigod, kill me. Just shoot me right now."

Dillon pulls out his phone. Abbey says, "If you're calling Dani, put the call on speaker."

He does, and Dani answers with, "Where are you?"

"Home."

"Long lunch, Dillon. When you asked for an extra hour, did you know you'd be gone all day?"

"Not really."

"Good, because this private eye adventure is pure adrenalin. Like crack for the senses. I'd hate for you to miss out on all the fun."

"Were you busy?"

"Let me put it this way: I've had exactly one call since you left. And no appointments. But let's talk about you. What's up? Why are you calling?"

"Um...I was just wondering...uh...did you happen to come by my place today?"

Dani pauses. "Why do you ask?"

Abbey sets her jaw and whispers, "She took it! I *knew* it!"

Dillon says, "I had something here, and it's missing."

"Wow. Thanks, Dillon. You've misplaced something, so your first thought is to accuse me of breaking into your home and stealing it?"

"You've got a key."

"True enough. But still. Why would you accuse me?"

"Because you're the only one who knows where I hide the files and stuff you don't want to keep at the office."

"I see. Can I ask *you* a question?"

"Uh..."

"Who's Doug Ballard?"

Dillon looks at Abbey and frowns. "Um...Doug *Ballard?*"

Dani says, "The friend you were doing work for? The one who paid you the thousand bucks last month? The one I asked you about after finding the entry on our Profit and Loss statement?"

"Oh. Right. He's—"

"Don't lie to me, Dillon. It'll change everything between us."

Seeing Abbey shaking her head "no" he says, "I'd rather not say."

Dani says, "You don't need to. I can put two and two together."

"What do you mean?"

"It's math. Two and two. The answer's four."

"So?"

"From the echo I can tell you're on speaker phone."

"I'm always on speaker."

"You've already admitted you're at your place."

Dillon sighs. "Are you getting ready to do that whole Sherlock Holmes routine?"

"You better believe it, only this time you're gonna listen." She pauses. Then says, "Um...where was I?"

"You've caught me on speaker phone in my own home. As usual. Want to impress me? Tell me what I'm wearing."

"Don't try to distract me. Yes, you're always on speaker phone, but this time you're not playing *Shadows of the Damned*, or whatever, or I'd hear screaming zombies self-mutilating in the background."

"*Shadows* has demons, not zombies. And anyway—"

"Hush, Dillon! My *ah-ha!* moment approaches. The fact you're home, on speaker, and *not* playing video games tells me you're not alone. Someone's with you. Someone who wants to hear our conversation. And since I know everyone in your circle of life other than the mysterious Doug Ballard, I can only assume he's the one sitting beside you that has a vested interest in whatever we have to say."

"Are you pacing the floor?" Dillon says. "You usually pace the floor when you think you're Sherlock."

Dani says, "You *wish* I was pacing the floor!"

"I do? Why?"

"Never mind. Forget that part. But you might be interested to know I recently ran a search on Doug Ballard and discovered that no such person in your age group resides in the states of Tennessee or Kentucky."

"So?"

"You've left me no choice but to deduce that Doug is a complete fabrication: an alias you created to throw me off the scent. And the only reason you'd do that is to protect Doug's true identity. So I had to ask myself, 'What possible reason could Dillon have for protecting this guy's identity?' And the reason is simple: your so-called 'friend' is a female, and one you fancy. And as I pause to contemplate all the females in Nashville you could be drawn to whose identity you need to protect, I can only come up with one name: Abbey Rayne." She pauses, then says, "Hello, Abbey."

Abbey says, "You can't possibly have determined that from whatever the fuck you just said."

"Well, it's possible I was nudged to that conclusion because of the hotel room you and Dillon shared earlier today."

"*What?*" Dillon gasps. "You *followed* us?"

"Of course not."

"Who did? Fanny?"

"Don't be ridiculous. I can't even get her to show up for *work.*"

"Then how'd you know where I went?"

229

"You might remember me saying I received one phone call after you left the office today? That's your clue. By the way, congratulations on the hotel thing. I'm proud of you both. And now that the secret's out, can I ask what project you've been helping Abbey with? Maybe I can help."

"No thanks." Abbey says, trying to maintain her cool. But Dillon can't help but notice her eyes are smoldering. As her anger reaches the boiling point her words fairly explode: "You had no right to take that box!"

To which Dani responds, "Wait. You know about the box? Whoa! This sheds a whole new light on the situation."

Which makes Dillon say, "Dani? Don't you dare open it."

"How can I not?" she says.

"If you do, I'll walk away. I'll never speak to you again."

"Relax. I'm in your driveway. Let's chat. You too, Abbey."

Chapter 22

TO DILLON'S GREAT EMBARRASSMENT, the first words out of Abbey's mouth are: "We didn't have sex."

"You *didn't?*" Dani says. "Wow, what a shock!"

"Why are you being so *mean?*" Dillon says.

"You really want to know? I'm *pissed* at you, Dillon! If Abbey knows about the box it's obviously hers, which means she talked you into holding it."

"So what? I hold things for *you* all the time."

"Did it never occur to you the box contains evidence that can be used against her in a *murder* investigation? I can't believe you'd let her put you in that type of situation."

Abbey says, "That's a horrible thing to say. Dillon and I are friends."

"Then how about the three of us open the box together?"

"Where is it?"

"In the trunk."

To Dillon's complete shock, Abbey removes a gun from her handbag and points it at Dani's face. "Show me," she says.

Dani looks at Dillon. "Let's not bring her home to meet your parents."

Chapter 23

DANI POPS THE TRUNK; shows Abbey the box. Abbey leaves it there and closes the trunk, saying, "It's not what you think."

"I believe you. Because if you had to point a gun at my face it's obviously *far* worse than I thought."

Abbey sighs. "Drive me to my car?"

"Where is it?"

"Green Tree Mall."

"Do I have a choice?"

"Not really. But on the way, I'll tell you what's in the box if you tell me about the phone call you got today."

Dani shakes her head. "You don't need a gun to make *that* trade."

As Dani backs her car out of the driveway she says, "About an hour after Dillon left, my friend Sophie called. Her Uncle Sal has connections to...certain people downtown, and one of them called him and said two detectives followed Abbey Rayne and her boyfriend to the Hampton Inn and had requested a search warrant for the boyfriend's house. Sal recognized Dillon's name and address from a list Sofe gave him last year. He called her, she called me, and I hauled ass to Dillon's house while you and Dillon were still at the hotel."

"What kind of list does this man have?"

Dillon says, "Dani's life gets threatened from time to time, so Sofe gave Uncle Sal a list of names and addresses she wanted him to protect. I'm on the list."

"And who's Uncle Sal?"

"Sal Bonadello, the crime boss?"

"Uncle Sal sounds like a valuable friend to have."

Dani says, "You might remember that, next time you pull a gun on me."

"I will. But I'll also remember you lied to me. You *did* have connections to a hitman after all."

"Yes. But that would have been a poor choice."

Abbey looks down at the gun in her lap and says, "Sorry about this."

"No problem, except I may have peed my pants."

Abbey laughs.

"You agreed to tell us what's in the box. Did you mean it?"

"What choice do I have? The minute I get out of the car you'll ask Dillon what I hired him to do last month, and when he tells you, you're gonna jump to all the wrong conclusions and make it worse than it is."

"Try me."

"I hired him to research the names, addresses, and Facebook pages of the parents of college students who raped multiple coeds."

"Here in town?"

"Several places."

"Why the parents?"

"I wanted to shatter their lives the way their sons shattered mine and the other girls'."

"How?"

"By threatening to publicly expose their sons."

Dani thinks on it a moment. Then says, "You obviously have some sort of evidence they haven't seen."

"Not really. Just the names and dates, and very convincing videos of the girls describing the events."

"None of which would stand up in court, as you've learned."

"Correct. Except that if I were to release the videos on YouTube and their Facebook pages the whole world would know what their sons did."

"They'd track it to you."

"That was my biggest concern. Obviously, I was hoping to find a way to avoid that."

"Want to know what I think?"

Abbey shrugs.

"I think you were planning to blackmail the parents."

Abbey smiles. "You're good."

Dillon, clearly surprised, says, "Why?"

"Because they're the ones who turn a blind eye to their sons' behavior. They're the ones who make financial contributions and hire attorneys and threaten lawsuits."

Dani says, "They're also the ones with the money."

"There's that."

"Why wouldn't the parents simply turn you in to the police?"

"I was hoping they wouldn't learn my identity."

"You were going to use a false name and wear a disguise?"

Abbey nods.

Dani says, "So I assume Tommy Kern's parents aren't on your list."

Dillon says, "They should be *first* on the list!"

Dani says, "She couldn't have approached them. They would have recognized her in a heartbeat." She slows the car suddenly, to avoid hitting a squirrel. When it passes, she speeds up and feels her tire roll over a second one.

"Shit!" she says, stopping the car. "We should go back."

Dillon looks out the back window. "No need to. He's dead."

Dani sighs heavily. "That's my second."

"Second squirrel?" Abbey says.

"Second road kill. I'm officially a serial killer."

"It's a club with many members," Abbey says.

"I should stop driving altogether. I'm a danger to society."

"Don't give up just yet," Abbey says, lifting her gun slightly for emphasis.

Dani puts the car in drive and continues their journey. After a few minutes she says, "Here's the problem with your plan: if the parents tell the police you interviewed the girls on camera, the police would find and question them. They'd reveal your identity and the police would arrest you."

"I didn't say it was a perfect plan."

When Dani comes to the next stop light, she stares into Abbey's eyes. Then says, "The girls were in on it."

Dillon says, "What do you mean?"

"She was planning to share the blackmail proceeds with the girls. In return, they'd protect her identity."

Abbey says, "I hoped it wouldn't come to that. As long as I wasn't greedy, and the parents understood the tapes could be all over the Internet within minutes, I didn't think they'd tell the police."

Dani says, "By paying you a reasonable amount now, they could avoid ruining their son's reputations forever."

"That's right."

"How much were you hoping to get?"

"Fifty grand."

"Each? Wow!"

"You're not horrified?"

Dani says, "Horrified? Please! I once caught a client's wife shoving her husband's toothbrush into her boyfriend's ass, then watched her put it back in the holder for her husband to use."

"Eew!"

"Another time I had to sit in a dentist's waiting room for twenty minutes watching *The View*! So no, I'm not horrified. In fact, I think fifty grand would have been a fair price. The problem is the sons would still get to stay in school, and they'd continue assaulting coeds."

"Which they'll do either way." She pauses. "Does that mean you'll keep my secret?"

"Let's just say I'm on your side, Abbey, like I've always been." As she turns into the mall parking lot she says, "Where's your car?"

Abbey directs her, but before getting out says, "You keep insisting you're on my side."

"It's true."

"Then why'd you tell the cops about the hitman?"

"I felt a legal obligation to report it."

"You had to know I wasn't serious."

"You seemed awfully serious at the time."

"I was traumatized, Dani. People say things when they're angry and frustrated. Tommy Kern beat the shit out of me and raped me, and got a legal dream team and support from the college, and I was on my own. In the preliminary hearing they dressed him up like a choir boy and no one cared that he broke my eye socket and gave me hyphema and double vision from an orbital blowout fracture. The doctor thought I'd been hit by a baseball bat! Then the whole fucking school turned against me! I'm not comparing my situation to yours. I wasn't kidnapped and abused for weeks like you were. But after your ordeal, everyone was on your side. People cared what happened to you, and wanted to help you. The whole world reached out to you. But I lost my scholarship, my friends, and until recently hundreds of students harassed me wherever I went. Do you have any idea what it's like to go to a ball game or simply walk into the student cafeteria and have half the people publicly boo you?"

"No."

"The system sucks, Dani. The people in power protect the colleges so the money can keep pouring in. The administration, parents, fraternities, local police, and judges are all working together to minimize the scandals, hiding behind phrases like "Look how she was dressed," or "She had it coming," or, "She should have known better." No one cares about the girls who've been abused. If they did they wouldn't allow repeat rapists to roam their campuses."

"I get all that, Abbey, and I agree with you 100%. But I'd hate to see you go to jail after all you've been through."

"Me too," Abbey says. "Which is why I never would have gone through with it. I simply don't have the guts." She looks at Dani and smiles. "But don't you love the idea?"

Dani smiles back. "Forcing the parents to compensate you and the others for what their sons have done and will *continue* doing? Of course. Because it's as close to justice as you're likely to get."

"I know, right? Because if their sons weren't getting away with raping girls, there'd be no one to blackmail in the first place."

Dillon asks Dani if it would have worked.

"I don't know. Possibly." She looks at Abbey. "But you're making the right decision not to try. What will you do with the box?"

"My uncle works at a vehicle recycling company. I'll get him to sneak it in one of the cars before crushing it."

"So it's safe to say the blackmail plot is behind us?" Dani asks.

Abbey sighs. "It was over before it started."

"It's the right decision, Abbey."

"I know."

Part Three: Dani Ripper

Chapter 1

"TELL ME AGAIN WHAT we're doing?" Sofe says.

"Looking for someone to interview. Be vigilant," I say. "Eyes sharp."

"What am I looking for, specifically?"

"Typically, I'd say bad lighting, and a guy who's bald, or parts his hair on the right side."

"Why?"

"Because in the movies the bad, weak, or stupid guys are always shown with poor lighting and part their hair on the right side. But since we're outside, the lighting won't come into play."

"I'm pretty sure that hair thing isn't very accurate."

"It's okay, I wouldn't expect you to understand. I'm the detective here, after all."

"*Private* detective."

"Whatever."

We look up and down the street, but see no one. Sofe says, "Give me an example of the hair thing."

"You remember when Christopher Reeve played Superman? He parted his hair on the left. But as Clark Kent, he parted it on the right, so he'd look geeky, weak, and awkward."

"I don't remember that."

I smile. "Which is a perfect example of why you need me in these types of situations."

"Except that we're in real life, not the movies."

"Which is a perfect example of why I need *you*!"

"There's one!" she says, pointing across the street at a man retrieving his newspaper from the porch.

"Good eye, Sofe!"

They watch as he glances at the headlines, then goes back inside.

Sofe says, "You said bald, right?"

"I did."

"This guy wasn't bald. Just balding."

"Yeah, but did you notice the lighting? Bad!"

"He was on a porch."

"Hips don't lie."

"What's that mean?"

"Nothing. I just like to say it."

We drive across the street and park in his driveway.

Sofe says, "What's the plan?"

"We're gonna interview him."

"Why?"

"He might have seen something."

"No. I mean why am *I* here instead of Dillon?"

"I already told you: Dillon's too close to Abbey."

"Dillon *loves* you."

"Oh yeah? Well, he loves her more. He'd probably slit my throat if she asked him."

"I sincerely doubt that."

"When it comes to love, you never know."

"Does that mean you'd slit Dillon's throat if I asked you?"

"Don't be silly."

She frowns. "Are you really going to sit there and tell me Dillon loves Abbey more than you love me?"

"Of course not. But we already *have* each other, so any throat-slitting would have happened back when you were hoping to get me to like you. Or vice-versa. Still, I shudder to think what Dillon might do if he thought it would win her over."

"You're totally overreacting. We're talking about Dillon, remember? I doubt he'd even wash his bed sheets for a girl. So anyway, you wanted to interview the Chapmans, to see if Abbey tried to blackmail them, but they're not home. So now we're across the street in their neighbor's driveway. What do you hope to learn from *this* guy?"

"I want to know if he's seen a girl who resembles Abbey, or if he's seen her car in the Chapmans' driveway. Stuff like that."

"Abbey's not your client. Why do you care if she's been blackmailing parents?"

"Because I think she's lying, and I hate not knowing stuff."

"Okay, I get that, but I'm confused. Didn't you tell me just last night that Abbey explained what was in the box and what she'd been up to?"

"Yup."

"And you said you were satisfied with her explanation."

"I was. But this morning I woke up with a funny feeling, so I decided to check out what she said about her uncle working at a vehicle recycling company."

"He doesn't?"

"Nope."

"Where *does* he work?"

"Fifth third Bank."

"Could she have another uncle? Or a family friend she *calls* her uncle?"

"Of course. But none that I could find."

She gives me a suspicious look. "Did you try very hard?"

"Nope."

"Because you wanted to do this whole detective surveillance thing, right?"

I grin.

Sofe shakes her head. "Only you."

A moment later she says, "Are you sure the Chapmans have a son in college?"

"Positive. Why?"

"Tuition's expensive. And these houses aren't very nice."

"Drew's on an athletic scholarship."

"Right. But I can't imagine the Chapmans could afford to pay Abbey fifty thousand dollars."

"You might be right. She may not have approached them."

"Then why start with them?"

"Convenience. They're the closest to my office."

"But they were definitely on the list you stole from Dillon's office?"

"Yes. But I didn't steal it. I borrowed it, copied it, and put it back in his desk drawer."

Sofe laughs. "If there's a world championship for hair-splitting, you'd get the gold medal."

"Thanks. Wanna come with me to meet the bald guy?"

"No."

"Suit yourself. But you'll be missing out on seeing a professional in action."

"Exactly what will I be missing?"

"You know those online lessons I've been watching? *How to Be the Best Private Detective Ever?* They offer free lessons hoping you'll buy the entire course. I haven't pulled the trigger yet, since it's like $300. But I'm learning a lot."

"Is this the one with that Scotch Tape guy?"

I frown. "His name—as you know quite well—is *Scott Tape*. Not Scotch. And everyone calls him Great Scott."

"So he says."

"Yes, and I believe him, since he's obviously great at what he does."

"Selling private eye courses? Super. And this affects us how?"

"I've mastered his lesson on how to interview the suspect's neighbors."

"Then please do so, before they call the cops."

"Why would they do that?"

"We've been sitting in their driveway for ten minutes."

"Oh. Right. Good point."

"Then...off you go! Go get 'em, tiger!"

I grin. "I'm on it."

"So *go* already!"

"Why are you rushing me?"

"I want that latte you promised."

I take a deep breath, then head for the door.

Great Scott says the best way to get a neighbor to let me in the door is knock on it, and when he answers, I should give my name, tell him I'm a P.I., and say, "I'd like to ask you a few questions about your neighbor. May I join you?" Great Scott says that will pique his interest because everyone wants to either gossip about his neighbors, or hear what they're up to. Then he says—Great Scott says this, not the neighbor—I should break eye contact, and start wiping my feet on the door mat, to send the subliminal message I'm about to enter the door. The neighbor will pick up on this subconsciously, and let me in.

I keep all this in mind as I knock on the door, as well as Great Scott's advice to be highly suspicious of everything I see and hear upon gaining entrance to a person's home.

The door opens. A lady appears and says, "Who are you?"

I smile. "Dani Ripper. I'm a Private Detective, and I'd like to ask you a few questions about your neighbors."

I break eye contact, and look for the door mat. There isn't one, so I start wiping my feet on the concrete floor where I assume the door mat should be.

"Which neighbor?" she says.

I say nothing, just keep wiping my feet, and wonder why she hasn't invited me in yet. Then I remember the part I left out. With my head still down, I say, "May I join you?"

"Not if your feet are *that* filthy."

I stop wiping my feet and look up at her. "They're clean."

"You sure?"

I nod.

"Show me."

"What do you mean?"

She points to my shoes. "Show me."

I take my shoes off and show her the bottoms. She takes them from me and frowns as she studies them. "How tall are them heels?"

"Five inches."

She frowns again. "They look new."

"They are."

"How much they set you back?"

I nearly tell her, but stop myself, because in a previous lesson Great Scott advised me not to tell civilians anything about myself that might alienate us, or brand me as an outsider. Since my shoes probably cost as much as her car, I say, "They were a gift."

"From a man?"

"A friend."

She gives me the same look of suspicion I'm supposed to be giving her. So I say, "May I ask you a few questions?"

"About my neighbor?"

"Yes."

"Which one?"

"Excuse me?"

"Which neighbor you want to ask about?"

That throws me for a loop. But I recover quickly, saying, "Does it matter?"

She shrugs.

"May I come in?"

"I reckon. By the way, I'm Millie."

"Nice to meet you."

As Millie opens the door I walk in proudly, and wonder what type of mark Great Scott would give me for this first attempt. Then I remember in his very first on-line lesson he said, "Don't expect me to give you a grade unless you've purchased the course."

Millie says, "You want me to get my husband?"

"If it's not too much trouble."

Since Great Scott won't grade a free student, I take a moment to grade myself. Yes, I botched the opening, but feel I showed exceptional resourcefulness in getting back on track. I decide to give myself an A. After all, the goal was to gain entry, and here I am.

Millie's husband rounds the corner, takes one look at me and says, "Holy *shit!* Who are *you?*"

"Dani Ripper, Private Detective."

"You with the police?"

Millie frowns. "She's a *private* detective, Idiot. Now put your tongue back in your mouth before she finds out you're a registered sex offender."

He says, "My name's Bing. Bing Adams."

I show him an expression so skeptical it would make Great Scott proud. Then I say, "That's an unusual name."

"Adams?" he says.

"Bing."

He shrugs. "My parents were Bing Crosby fans."

"And yet they named you Adams."

He and Milly give each other a look I deem unusually suspicious. Especially now that I see a giant Confederate flag hanging on their living room wall, behind the couch.

Noting my look, Bing says, "What's wrong?"

"I'm surprised you still have that."

"Why wouldn't we?"

"It's illegal, isn't it?"

"Who says?"

"I thought the government was making everyone get rid of these sorts of flags."

"Why?"

"It's been all over the TV."

"What are they sayin' about my flag?"

"It's offensive."

"To who?"

I almost correct his grammar, but don't, since that would identify me as an outsider. So I simply say, "I don't remember all the details, but my understanding is these flags can only be shown in museums."

"Our house *is* a museum."

"It *is*?" I glance around the room.

Millie says, "When people come to see 'em."

"Excuse me?"

Bing sings, "We really are a scree-um."

Then they both sing, "The Addams Family."

As Millie and Bing dance around the room laughing and high-fiving each other I realize I've lost control of the situation. Millie ushers me out the door, and I make a mental note to send Great Scott the full $300 this very afternoon.

I stand there a moment, then knock on the door again.

When Millie opens it, I say, "Can I have my shoes back?"

She says, "What shoes?"

Chapter 2

"THAT BITCH STOLE MY SHOES!"

"Are you sure about that?" Sofe says. "Because I saw you give them to her."

"That was just to get in."

"That was part of Great Scott's lesson?"

"No. It's...never mind."

"You can't just let her keep your shoes."

"I know. But she's not alone. Her husband's in on it with her. I think he's a registered sex offender."

"Eew. You think the shoes are for—"

"Oh God no! I mean, I *hope* not! I think they're just thieves. They've probably got a hundred pairs of stolen shoes in their closet."

"I can't believe you willingly handed over a pair of Manolos."

"Me either. But what can I do about it? Millie will claim I was barefoot when I got there. It'll be my word against hers."

"Millie?"

"The shit-brained, frickin' shoe thief."

"I dare you to say that five times quickly without screwing up."

"What?"

"The shit-brained frickin' shoe thief."

I try, and can't even say it twice. But what I *can* say is, "I wish I'd brought my gun."

Sofe frowns. "If you had, I wouldn't be here. Surely you haven't forgotten what happened last time?"

"With you? Or Dillon? Or do you mean that time I nearly shot Fanny?"

"Take your pick. But let me ask you something."

"What?"

"What would happen if Millie and her husband stole Callie *Carpenter's* shoes?"

"They'd already be dead."

"Okay, then."

I look at her. "Okay then, what? You think I'm gonna blow up their house over a pair of shoes?"

"Callie would."

"Fine. You want to help me blow their house up?"

"Nope."

"Do you even have the first idea *how* to blow up a house?"

"Shockingly, no. But Uncle Sal might."

"Should we call him?"

"That depends."

"On what?"

"How important are those Manolos to you?"

"Critically important. I'd do anything to get them back."

She raises an eyebrow. "Would you be willing to owe Uncle Sal a favor?"

"Uh...no. *Hell* no!"

She laughs. "You say her husband's a sex offender?"

"Millie said it. But she might have been kidding."

"Doesn't matter. Follow me."

"Where?"

"Just follow me."

She gets out of the car, and I follow her onto the porch. She knocks on the door. Bing answers, saying, "My wife already told you we don't know nothin' about them shoes."

Sofe says, "We can do this one of two ways."

"Let me guess: is one of them the hard way?"

"Yup."

"Tell me about that one."

"Have you ever heard of Sal Bonadello, crime boss of the Midwest United States?"

"What about him?"

"He's my uncle."

"So?"

"One call from me and Sal will blow your house down like the big bad wolf he is."

"I don't believe you."

She removes her phone from the back pocket of her jeans and presses a button. When Sal answers, she puts him on speaker and says, "Uncle Sal? You remember my friend Dani?"

"Sure!" he says. "A real beauty! Don't tell your Aunt Marie, but I see her in my dreams sometimes. What about her?"

"Some guy just stole her shoes."

"The *fuck*? What guy?"

Bing's face drops. He whispers, "Easy way!"

Sofe says, "Wait. There's been a new development. I think he's going to give her shoes back."

"Give me his address. I'll blow his fuckin' house down anyway."

"Thanks, Sal. But I'm pretty sure he's seen the error of his ways."

"That ain't how it works. We can't just let him slide on this—whatcha call—incident. It shows a lack of respect. When a man steals Dani's shoes it's the same as stealin' my shoes. And no fuckin' man steals *my* shoes, you understand?"

Bing says, "Mr. Bonadello? I didn't *steal* her shoes, I *found* them. The whole thing was a huge misunderstanding. I'm getting her shoes right now."

"What else you got?"

"Excuse me?"

"This whole thing smells, and I ain't talkin' about the shoes. My niece's friend needs—whatcha call—restitution. Where's Dani?"

"Right here, Uncle Sal."

"Does this piece of shit own anything your sweet little heart desires besides your shoes?"

"Yes sir."

"Name it."

"He's got a Confederate flag."

"I ain't givin' you that flag!" Bing says.

"Dani?"

"Yes sir?"

"Give me this bastard's address. I'll get your shoes, the flag, and something nice for Sophie, too, for her trouble. Then I'll cut his nuts off and tack 'em to that giant pine tree at our lake house so I can compare 'em to the others. He got a wife?"

"Yes sir."

"Good. I'll grind her knucklebones into dice for my next craps tournament."

"Thank you, Uncle Sal. His address is—"

Bing falls to his knees and starts begging for his life.

By the time Sal finishes with him I've got my shoes, the flag, and a pledge to contribute $5,000 and another Confederate flag to Sal's charity, *The Mothers of Sicily*. As we start to leave, Bing says, "What was the easy way?"

Sofe smiles. "Dani and I were going to show you our tits."

I look at her. "*What?*"

"You said you'd do anything to get them back."

"Yeah, but—"

Bing says, "It ain't right, givin' up my flag and five grand I don't even *have* yet. I ought to get *somethin'* out of it."

"Tell you what: next time you steal my shoes, I'll show you my tits. How's that?"

He frowns. Then says, "Why'd you knock on our door in the first place?"

Sofe and I look at each other. "I wanted to ask you about your neighbors, the Chapmans."

"What about 'em?"

"Hang on a sec."

I go to the car, get the computer images from my hand-bag, show him the first one. "Have you ever seen this car parked in the Chapman's driveway or on the street?"

He studies it a moment. "Nope."

"You're sure?"

"Yup."

I show him Abbey's photo. "How about her? Ever seen her at the Chapmans'?"

He looks at it a moment, and smiles. "Is it worth ya'll showin' your tits?"

I look at Sofe.

"Not to me," she says.

Bing looks at me. "How 'bout *you*, sugar plum?"

Sofe says, "If she does that, and your information's bo-gus, Uncle Sal will absolutely kill you."

"I understand."

They look at me.

I frown, take a deep breath, and hoist my shirt and bra up to my neck. I count three seconds, then end the show, and the only evidence anything happened is the long, thick rope of drool leaking from the corner of Bing's mouth, hanging halfway to the floor. He waits till it falls, then says, "I saw a girl who sorta looked like this one, 'cept she had short, black hair."

"Could it have been a wig?"

"It *was* a wig, but I didn't know that till later. Anyway, what struck me as weird, this gal didn't drive, she *walked* to their house, rang the doorbell, went inside for an hour, then came out on the porch and talked to the Chapmans some more. I got a good look at her 'cause the light was on. After a few minutes she walked away in the dark. That's what I remember most: I thought it was dangerous to walk in this neighborhood at night."

"When was this?"

"Three weeks ago."

As Sofe and I start walking to my car he calls out, "I gotta say, I think you done pulled a bait-and-switch on me. What I thought was tits turned out to be 60% padded bra."

Tough shit! I say to myself, and keep walking.

He adds, "Your lumps are well-formed, but too small, you don't mind my sayin' so."

I don't give a shit what a shoe thief-slash-registered sex offender thinks about my "lumps", so I say nothing and keep walking.

Then he says, "I'd rather see your friend's tits."

Who wouldn't? I think.

As Sofe and I get to the car and reach for our respective door handles, he raises his voice and says, "If this is about the "Chapmans getting' blackmailed, I got more to tell."

Sofe and I stop dead in our tracks, turn, and look at him.

Bing says, "What I'm sayin', I got somethin' to tell if your friend's got somethin' to show."

Sofe and I look at each other.

I say, "What do you think?"

She studies my face a moment, then says, "What's it worth to you?"

Chapter 3

IT WAS WORTH GETTING my promise to play Countdown.

Tonight, at O'Shea's restaurant.

Which is where we are, right now.

But before we start the game, let me catch you up on what Bing told us after Sofe flashed her boobs at him and Millie (Why Millie? Because unlike me, Sofe has a rack that would put a 12-point buck to shame, and Millie wasn't gonna let her husband view it unattended).

After drooling from both sides of his mouth, Bing said Cathy Chapman told Millie that the girl in the short black wig clipped them for $50,000 after showing a video of her son having sex with a drunk college girl. She said the sex was consensual, but Cathy was afraid her son would be kicked off the team and lose his scholarship. I asked how they managed to come up with that much money so quickly, and Bing said they tapped into the line of credit they had planned to use for a home renovation.

To recap, Abbey didn't show the Chapmans a video of a rape victim being *interviewed*, she showed them a *sex* video!

But I don't buy the whole drunk-consensual part. I think somehow Abbey managed to film frat boys raping girls. Then she went to their parents, showed them the videos, and asked for fifty grand to destroy the videos.

Brilliant.

So here we are at O'Shea's, and despite my great trepidation at playing this crazy game I recently invented, the look on Sophie's face is priceless: she's literally beaming.

"Ground rules," she says.

"We take turns making each other do sexy things while sitting at the table. Every task has to be completed within 60 seconds, hence the name *Countdown*. If you fail to complete the task within 60 seconds, or get kicked out of the restaurant, you lose."

"Can we refuse to do the task?"

"Yes, but if you tell me to do something and I refuse, you have to do the same task in order to win. And if you fail or refuse to do it, I automatically win."

She smiles broadly. "I *love* it, Dani!"

"Really?"

"Yes! I'm really proud of you for coming up with this."

I give her a look. "Go easy on me, okay?"

She grins. Then says, "Let's be clear about the punishments. Spell out exactly what I'm allowed to make you do after you lose."

"*If* I lose."

She rolls her eyes. "Whatever." Then says, "So, what does the winner get to do?"

"The winner can make the loser do anything she wants, with two exceptions."

Sofe frowns. "You didn't say anything about exceptions."

"They're reasonable: first, whatever the winner asks, the loser only has to do it for an hour."

"That *is* reasonable. What's the second exception?"

"It can't involve my butthole."

She laughs so loudly the customers around us are staring. Then she says, "If you get a personal exemption, I should have one, too."

"Okay."

"My punishment can't involve living things."

"What do you mean?"

"I don't want tarantulas crawling over my naked body, or gerbils stuffed up my—"

"*SOPHIA RENEE ALEXANDER!*" I shout.

"What?"

"You can't be *serious!*"

"I am. No living things."

"I mean, why would you even *think* I'd come up with that type of punishment?"

"Well, you said the winner could—"

"If this is how your mind works, I can't *imagine* what you might put me through. I'm sorry, Sofe, but this could get *way* out of hand. I can't do this."

I look at my plate a long time as neither of us says a word. But I can feel her staring at me, and know exactly what she's thinking: she showed her boobs to a pervert to get me to play a game I invented, and now I'm backing out. I don't know what to say, so I look up at her and tell the truth. "This was supposed to be fun."

She says, "It's a great game, Dani. We can salvage it."

"How?"

"All we have to do is tell each other what we're playing for, in advance."

"What do you mean?"

"I'll tell you right now what you have to do if you lose, and you'll tell me what I have to do if you win. And if we agree, we play. If we don't agree, we keep coming up with different punishments until we both agree."

I feel my face break into a genuine smile. "That's a *great* idea, Sofe!"

"You first," she says. "What will you make me do for up to an hour?"

"You'll have to give me a full body massage...with no funny stuff."

"Funny stuff?"

"No inappropriate touching."

She frowns. "Where's the fun in that?"

"It'll build the anticipation and get me in the mood."

"For what?"

I wink.

"Done!" she says. "Ready for mine?"

"Not really, but I'm bracing myself."

She tells me, and all I can say is, "Are you kidding me?"

"Nope. That's what I want you to do."

"What's the catch?"

"No catch."

"And I get to wear *clothes*?"

"Yes. As long as they're appropriate for the occasion."

I shrug. "You're on! Let's do this!"

We shake on it and she says, "Who goes first?"

"We flip a coin."

I produce a quarter, tell her to make the call. She laughs and says, "Tails, of course!"

I flip the coin, and it lands on heads. I place my phone on the table and set the timer to one minute. "Ready for your first challenge?"

"Lay it on me!" she says.

I lower my voice and say:

Chapter 4

"SEE THAT CUTE COUPLE in the booth?"

"How could I not? They're ten feet away."

"You have to stare at the guy for a full minute. You can't turn away. If he looks at you, you have to smile and flirt."

"For a whole minute?"

"Yeah. If he happens to notice you."

She chuckles. "You don't have a chance, Dani girl."

"Tell me when you're ready."

"I'm ready."

I press the key, and the countdown starts. Then I holler, "Stop *looking* at him!"

Of course the guy *and* his date turn to see what I'm talking about, and Sofe bursts out laughing, but keeps staring at him and winking, and making kissy lips, and within 15 seconds his girlfriend says, "Do you *mind?*"

Sofe keeps it up and the guy's trying to calm his date down, and she threatens Sofe, but Sofe won't take her eyes off the guy. She tosses in a couple of lip licks for good measure. After 45 seconds, the girlfriend gets to her feet and says, "I'm reporting you to the manager." Sofe keeps staring at him, and of course the minute ends long before the young lady comes back with the manager. When they approach the table, Sofe says, "Relax. I'm not interested in your man. We're gay."

"I don't believe you!" she says.

"Want me to kiss her right now?"

"Yes."

Sofe stands, and starts coming around the table.

The manager notes the customers staring at us and says, "Please don't. I'm sorry to disturb you."

The young lady says, "This is ridiculous."

The manager walks her back to her table and offers to comp the couple's dessert.

Sofe says, "You just made it tens times harder on yourself, because now everyone's going to be watching us."

"Getting nervous?" I say.

"Not at all. Ready for *your* challenge?"

"Yes. But remember, it has to be something you're willing to do if I refuse."

"No problem."

She sets the timer and says, "Unbutton the top two buttons of your blouse. When the waiter shows up to take our drink order, you'll have exactly one minute to get him to look down your blouse."

My face goes white. "I'm not wearing a bra!"

She smiles. "Exactly."

I think about it a moment. "How will I know if he looks? I mean, he won't look down my blouse if I'm *watching* him."

"Yes he will. But if you think it'll help you to close your eyes or look away I'll watch him for you and tell you. And yes, you can trust me to be honest. Are you in or out?"

I take a deep breath. "In."

She laughs. "This ought to be hilarious!"

Red-faced, I get through the challenge, though I bristled when the waiter approached and Sophie said, "Dani, your shirt's unbuttoned."

After he left I said, "You made it impossible for me to fail. Admit it: you *wanted* him to look!"

"I'll admit I'm having too much fun to stop after one challenge."

I smile. "You like my game."

"I *love* your game. They should put it on TV. I can't wait for my next challenge. If it's as lame as the first one, you've already lost."

I set the timer and smile. "That first one was to soften you up, make you overconfident."

"Uh huh."

"You underestimated me, Sofe."

"You think?"

"Yup, and now you'll have to pay the price. Make a note: this is where you lose."

"We'll see. Just remember your own rules: if I refuse, *you* have to do it. And if you don't, I win."

"No problem. I came prepared. Ready?"

"Let's hear it."

Chapter 5

"YOU'VE GOT 60 SECONDS to remove your panties and place them on the table!"

She gives me a look. "You're kidding."

"Nope." I laugh out loud at her expression.

"Dani."

"What?"

"You know I'm wearing designer jeans."

"*Are* you? I hadn't noticed."

She looks at me through new eyes and says, "You conniving little shit!"

I grin.

She says, "You *specifically* asked me to wear these pants!"

"Yup."

She imitates my voice: "'Oh, Sofe, *please* wear those skin-tight designer jeans! They're so *hot!*'"

"They *are!*"

"Uh huh. And I said, 'I can't wear pants if you're wearing a *dress*,' and you said, '*Please* Sofe! *Please* wear them! For *me?*'"

"And you did," I say.

"You set me up."

"Yup. So. Are you gonna accept the challenge, or do I have to remove mine to score the win?"

"I'll do it."

My eyes bug out. "You *will?*"

Sofe removes something from her handbag, places the large linen napkin over her lap and says, "Set the timer."

Working under the cloak of the napkin, she unbuttons and unzips her jeans without anyone noticing. Then she shows me what she took from her handbag: nail scissors. She uses them to cut both sides of her panties, then lifts her butt off her chair and tugs them off and places them on the table.

With eight seconds to spare.

She places the scissors back in her handbag and removes another item and my eyes go wide. "Ready for your second challenge?" she says.

Chapter 6

SOPHIE WON.

There was no way I was going to insert her Mini Bullet into my woohoo at the dinner table, even though she assured me it had been thoroughly sterilized and was well-known to be the quietest vibrator on the market.

After politely declining the challenge, I marveled at her willingness to not only perform it, but to do so at the highest speed setting. I was left hoping someone would figure out what she was doing and kick us out of the restaurant, but doubted that would happen within the allotted time. To hedge my bet I hollered, "Sofe! You can *not* use a dildo in a restaurant!"

But it didn't work. She was right about her bullet being crazy quiet, and when I made the comment she pretended to laugh and said, "That's hilarious! What a funny joke!"

So anyway, Sofe beat me at my own game, and you're probably wondering what she's gonna make me do.

Well, I'll tell you, but prepare to be surprised:

Chapter 7

SHE WANTS ME TO attend a 5th grade school play!

And, as requested, I'll dress appropriately for the occasion.

It's in two weeks, on a Friday night: November 6th.

I had to ask why.

"It's a secret," she says, and it was.

But I got it out of her a couple hours ago, and then we fell asleep crying in each other's arms.

Sofe has a daughter!

Happened ten years ago, when she was seventeen. Gave the baby to a friend of her parents, along with a promise to never contact the child till after she turns eighteen.

You might think you know all your lover's secrets, but you don't. After all we've meant to each other she waited till tonight to tell me this bombshell, and swears it's the last one she's kept from me, but I doubt that's true. I told her the same thing months ago, but was lying through my teeth. To this day I haven't told her a couple of huge ones, like...wait. Promise you won't tell?

Good. Here goes:

If you've been keeping track of my exploits the last couple of years you know my friend, Donovan Creed, once hired me to see if I could seduce Callie Carpenter, the assassin. Callie and I came close, but it didn't quite happen. Creed was thrilled, because it meant she was being faithful to him, and that's the reassurance he needed for their relationship to work.

But their relationship *didn't* work. Not because she cheated, but because they were terrible together.

But what you don't know—*bombshell alert!*—is this:

Callie and I had sex.

It didn't happen till after she and Creed broke up, and I wasn't pursuing her, wasn't even *thinking* about her back then, since I was dating Sophie's nemesis, the teacher, Beth Conroy. But yes, it happened. And what's worse...

Our relationship is ongoing.

Now you know why Callie's almost always available to come to my rescue when problems get out of hand. That said, Callie will probably end up being my biggest problem someday, since there appears to be no way to end things with her. She and I had a talk after Sofe and I got back together, but it didn't go well. I told her I was in love with Sofe, and had moved back in with her. Callie said, "No problem. If you truly love her I can accept it. I'll spare her life."

Whaaa?

Callie clarified as far as she's concerned, I can *love* Sofe, *live* with her, even *marry* her if I want...but if Callie comes to town and contacts me, I can either meet her or Sophie dies.

So yeah, we've met a few times, and no, it's not just sex. It's usually dinner and drinks and conversation and...

And *then* sex.

And while the sex is incredible—the type only a truly crazy person can offer—I like to tell myself I'm not cheating, I'm simply taking one for the team. My sexual sacrifice is keeping Sofe and her daughter alive.

But let's not tell Sofe. You know how she loves to turn things around and make them appear worse than they are.

As for her daughter?

She wants me to see her, and I can't wait. It'll be from a distance, but she wants me to do something more. After the performance, she wants me to work my way over to tell her how well she did. I'm not supposed to get all weird, I'm just supposed to say something like, "Hey, great job tonight, Zoey!" Then report whatever she says to Sofe, which will almost certainly be "Thank you."

But to Sofe they'll be words of gold.

"Eight more years," she said. "Then Zoey and I can finally build a relationship."

"If she wants to," I say reflexively, then wish I hadn't.

"Of course she'll *want* to!" Sofe says. "Why *wouldn't* she?"

"I don't know. It just came out."

"Why *wouldn't* she want to?"

"She will," I say, kissing her forehead.

"Damn straight she will!" Sofe says, and sounds totally convinced...till I leave her bedroom and hear her crying into her pillow.

Chapter 8

IT'S NOON. COLIN CHAPMAN, the alleged rapist, is walking toward me.

"You sounded kinda cute on the phone," he says, flashing killer dimples. "But...wow! You're gorgeous!"

"Thanks."

He pretends not to look me over and I pretend it's okay, but I'm not stupid. I know given half a chance this bastard would club me unconscious and drag me by the hair to Pound Town.

"You said you wanted to ask me about my parents?"

"Yes."

He smiles, waits politely for me to continue.

Colin's a piece of shit, but a charming one. I can see why girls are attracted to him. He lures them in, spikes their drinks, and...

"Ms. Ripper?"

"Huh? Oh. Sorry. Yes. I need a favor."

"For you, anything!"

"I'd like you to call your parents and tell them I need to meet them. They've been avoiding me."

"That doesn't sound like my parents. Especially my dad. No offense, but has he *seen* you?"

"No. I went to their house, but no one was home. Since then I've left three messages, but they haven't called me back."

"You said you're a private detective?"

"Yes."

"What's this about?"

"Believe it or not, I might be able to help them recover a sizeable amount of money."

"That sounds mysterious."

"It is."

"Give me a sec." He pulls his phone from his pocket, walks a few feet away, and calls his parents. After a moment he walks back and says, "Can you meet them in twenty minutes?"

"Yes."

"They'll be there."

"Thank you."

"Can I come?"

"No."

He laughs, says, "Yes I can," and I realize he made a joke: he can cum. Hilarious.

He says, "I'm just kidding. I've got classes and practice. I'm on the team."

I know I'm supposed to swoon or something. Since I don't, he adds, "First string, varsity. Ever been to one of my games?"

Can you *believe* this guy? One of *his* games? Not the team's?

"No."

"You should come Saturday, one o'clock. It's gonna be a great one. Afterward, maybe we can—"

I put my hand up to stop him. With thousands of possible sarcastic responses available to me, I'm surprised to hear myself say, "I'm too old for you."

Of course that was a stupid thing to say, because he immediately protests, and I can tell this fuckwad is used to having his way with women to the extent he can already visualize adding the Dani Ripper crotch notch to his bedpost. So I stop him again and say, "Colin, listen to me. I'm not saying my age of 25 is too old for you. I'm saying *I'm* too old for you. I won't let you get me drunk, or drug me, or lure me to a secluded place where you can beat the piss out of me. You'll never get in my pants. It'll never happen."

"Never say never, pretty lady."

"Never! ...Never! ...Never!"

"Funny."

"Never! ...Never! ...Never! ...*NEVER!*"

Chapter 9

BEN AND CATHY CHAPMAN are surprisingly cordial.

After offering me the nicest seat in their den, Cathy gets right to it: "Colin said you might have found some money for us?"

"A better way to phrase it is I might be able to get a size-able refund on your recent purchase."

They look at each other curiously, but no large purchase comes to mind. Then they remember I'm a private detective and their excitement turns to concern. That's my cue to say "Colin's been naughty again."

"What do you mean?" Cathy says, tentatively.

"He's been carrying a concealed weapon without a permit."

"Colin has a *gun?*"

"Worse: he has a penis. And he's been using it to assault a number of young ladies on campus. Please don't insult me by denying it, since I know you recently paid $50,000 to make this problem go away."

"That's ridiculous!"

"You don't remember watching a video recently? The one where Colin was raping one of his young friends?"

"*Friends?*"

"I'm trying to be civil."

Ben says. "You just accused our son of being a *rapist!*"

"I didn't *accuse* him. I stated it as a fact."

Cathy says, "We don't know what you're talking about. Colin's an honor student. He's made the Dean's List five times. He's a member of the debate team, co-captain of the football team, and one of the most highly-respected boys in the entire college!"

"Wow. You must be so proud."

"We are."

"You're selling him short, though. He's also an accomplished rapist."

Ben says, "You lied your way into our home to tell us *this?*"

"I didn't lie. I honestly believe I can recover a substantial portion of the blackmail payment you made."

Ben says, "We didn't pay any blackmail."

"Let her speak," Cathy says.

"Thanks Cathy. Here's the deal: I think I know who blackmailed you. What I don't know is what was on the video she showed you that convinced you to make the payment."

Ben says, "Are you with the police?"

"No."

"Are you wearing a wire?"

"You mean besides the underwire in my push-up bra?"

"Yes."

"No."

"Why should we believe you?"

"Because if I'm right about the young lady who black-mailed you I might be able to threaten her into giving the money back."

"What's in it for you?"

"Half of everything I recover."

Ben frowns. "Twenty-five *thousand?*"

"I think that's fair."

"Ten is fair."

I shake my head. Never fails. "Forget it," I say, getting to my feet.

"Wait!" Cathy says. "If you make her give back the money, what keeps her from releasing the video?"

"The threat of a jail sentence."

They look at each other. "I don't know," Ben says.

"How well do you know her?" Cathy says.

"I'm not sure I know her at all. I just got a description, put two and two together, and came up with four. I'm very good at math."

"If you confront this lady, what assurance would we have that Colin's scholarship and reputation won't be compromised?"

"I won't confront her unless I'm certain she'll play ball. And of course I'll convey that your utmost priority is for Colin to remain on campus so he can continue raping un-suspecting coeds for years to come."

"Thank you," Cathy says, as Ben and I look at her in disbelief.

She says, "Oh, stop it. You know what I meant."

Ben says, "How about you keep twenty and give us thirty?"

I have to work hard not to laugh in his face over his haggling. Obviously, I have no intention of asking Abbey to return a cent of their money. I just want to know exactly what she's up to, and figure this is the best way to find out. But since I'm playing a part, I say, "Fine. I'll give you 60% of whatever I recover."

"And how will we know you're telling the truth?"

I think a moment. "Good question."

I'm obviously not good at shakedowns, since this issue never crossed my mind. But of course they'd want to know. Otherwise, I could collect the full fifty and tell them she refused to pay.

I think about it some more, and come up with this: "I suppose you'll have to trust me."

"*Trust* you?"

"Yes."

"You *hate* our son! How could we possibly trust you?"

I shrug. "You trusted the girl who blackmailed you."

"That's different."

"How?"

"We had no choice."

"Let me put it this way: I didn't have to come here at all. I could have gone right to the blackmailer and demanded the money and you never would have known."

"True, but like you said, you don't know what was on the video."

"I have a good idea, after talking to Millie."

Ben gives his wife an angry look. Then says, "What do *you* think was on the video?"

"I think it contained undisputable evidence that Colin brutally raped a girl. I think the assault was so violent, even Colin's defense attorney wouldn't be able to argue the sex was consensual."

Ben takes a deep breath. "Close enough."

"Do we have a deal?"

"That sounds like something you'd say if you were wearing a wire."

"So we *don't* have a deal?"

"I won't answer that, nor will I admit to having been blackmailed. But surely you can look into our finances and determine what $50,000 represents to us."

"What are you saying?"

"I'm saying if you suddenly find yourself with a large sum of money and feel like sharing a portion with us, it would be greatly appreciated. But whatever you decide to do, please don't destroy Colin's life in the process."

This comment sets my teeth on edge and makes me want to slap the shit out of him, then slap him for shitting (I didn't invent that phrase, I heard Donovan Creed say it. And it's totally appropriate in this case). I know Ben's trying to protect his kid, but this statement goes so far beyond hypocrisy I feel my stomach roil.

So I say, "You should call Colin on the phone every afternoon and say the same thing: please don't destroy a young lady's life tonight."

He nods. "Duly noted."

They walk me to the door and hold it open for me.

Duly noted? I want to leave them with a biting, clever remark to let them know how pissed I am, but can't think of anything. So I stand there like an idiot with my brows knitted, and eventually walk out the door and hear it close behind me. I remain on their porch, recounting our conversation: they want to protect their son, but want their money back. And I'm not to destroy Colin's life in the process. But the bottom line is something Abbey knows full well: Colin will be allowed to remain in school with full scholarship, and Abbey won't. And Colin will continue raping other people's daughters, and will continue getting away with it.

It's too much.

I knock on their door again, and when they answer, I say, "Who's your mortgage with?"

"What mortgage?" Ben says.

"You didn't refinance your home?"

Cathy says, "Yes. Of course."

"Which bank?"

Ben looks at her. She stumbles, "Um..."

It takes her a couple of seconds to tell me, but by then I've already figured out what happened. "You got the money from athletic boosters."

She frowns. "What difference does it make? It was still our money."

I give them my dirtiest look and say, "Fuck you both!" Then leave them to wonder if I'm still on board or planning to do nothing.

Chapter 10

"ABBEY? IT'S DANI. Please call me at your earliest convenience."

Same message, same lack of response.

I walk into Dillon's office and ask "When's the last time you spoke to Abbey Rayne?"

"Whenever we dropped her off at the mall."

"That was a week ago. Surely you've called to check up on her since then."

"I have. Several times. But she never called me back."

"You're certain?"

"I wouldn't lie to you."

"Just to clarify, you're talking about the evening she pulled a gun on us."

"She aimed it at you, as I recall. But what's your point?"

"She's not answering my calls either."

"Why are *you* trying to contact her?"

"I did a little checking around."

288

"*Why?*" he says, clenching his jaw.

"I didn't believe her."

"About what?"

"Not having the guts to blackmail the parents."

"You can't possibly think she blackmailed them."

"I know she did. Colin Chapman's parents admitted it."

His face shifts from disbelief to anger. "So *what?* Who cares?"

"I just thought you should know."

"Why? What difference does it make?"

"I think she murdered Tommy Kern. Or had him murdered."

"She didn't."

"How can you be so sure?"

"I just know."

I stare at him before saying, "You know she doesn't love you."

"Wow. Thanks so much for telling me that."

"I just don't want your judgment clouded by the illusion she loves you."

"No danger of *that*, long as you're around."

I sigh. "You know I care about you."

He says nothing, so I say, "Dillon?"

"What?"

"You know I care about you...don't you?"

He frowns. "I guess."

"It may not seem like it right now, but I promise there's a perfect girl out there for you, and someday—"

"*Jesus*, Dani!"

"What?"

"Shut up!"

"I'm serious, Dillon. I honestly—"

"Please! Just shut up, okay?"

"Okay."

"*Jesus!*

We're quiet till I say: "If you know something, you need to tell me."

"Why? Because you're never gonna let it go?"

"Not if I think she murdered Tommy Kern."

"She didn't."

"So you say, but where's your proof?"

He pauses, then says, "What if her only crime is black-mailing the parents?"

"I don't give a shit about the blackmail, Dillon."

"You swear?"

"I hope she got a million dollars." The look on his face says it all: "I'll be damned," I say. "You knew!"

He shrugs.

"You fucking *knew*! Since when?"

"If we're talking about the blackmail, I've known since the day after we dropped her off at the mall."

"She told you?"

"Nope."

"Then you *didn't* know. You suspected."

"Nope. I knew."

I cock my head. "What're you saying exactly?"

"You remember the box she gave me to hold?"

I frown. "That's a stupid question. Yes, Dillon. I re-member the box. What about it?"

"I opened it."

I can't see my face, but my eyes couldn't possibly look bigger than they feel right now. "*When?*"

"I told you: the day after we dropped her off."

"But...*how?*"

"I figured out where she hid it."

"Where?"

He smiles. "*Now* who's the brilliant private eye?"

"Me. It's still me."

"Really? Then tell me where she hid it."

"It's obvious."

"You think?"

"Of course! Jesus, Dillon! It's so obvious a *child* could have figured it out."

"Then why didn't you?"

"I was too busy proving she blackmailed the parents."

"Me too. So I found the box, opened it, and learned the answers."

"Which answers?"

"The ones you'd know if you'd opened the box and watched the videos."

"You watched them?"

"I did."

"And?"

He says nothing.

"Come on, Dillon! What did you see!"

"Dozens of rapes, attempted rapes, and a bunch of consensual sex. The rapes were cross-referenced with names, dates, and the home and Facebook addresses I supplied."

"You still have the videos?"

"Of course."

"Did you find evidence of the blackmailing?"

"Lots. Including how much she got from each family."

"How much all together?"

"That I know of? Three hundred and fifty thousand."

"Holy shit!"

"I'm proud of her," he says.

"Me too. Was there any cash in the box?"

"Nope. Sorry."

"What about the murder? It was filmed, right?"

"Nope."

"You're certain?"

"Positive."

"So this whole thing was about the blackmail? Nothing else?"

"Nothing else."

"Swear to God?"

"I do."

"Then you won't mind letting me watch the videos."

"All of them?"

"Of course."

"There's a lot."

"Like what?"

"Dozens of thumb drives in pre-addressed envelopes, and also the laptop she used to live-stream the rapes into files."

"I'll start with the laptop."

"Okay."

"You're gonna give it to me? Just like that?"

"Of course."

I check his face for sincerity. Then say, "Thanks, Dillon."

"You're surprised?"

"Shocked."

He says, "By the way, Abbey's not getting your messages."

"How do you know?"

"She has a different number now. Want it?"

I nod.

He gives it to me, and I enter it into my contact list, call her, and leave the same message. Dillon opens his credenza cabinet, pulls out Abbey's laptop, hands it to me.

"Will you walk me through it?" I ask.

"Of course."

I stare at the keyboard a full minute. Then ask, "How do you turn it on?"

Chapter 11

ABBEY'S LAPTOP IS COMPLETELY BLANK. All the files have been erased.

I have to ask: "Why would you do that?"

"To protect her."

"She doesn't fucking love you, Dillon!"

"I know. But I love *her*."

"You let her get away with murder!"

"Blackmail."

"You honestly believe she didn't film the murder?"

"She didn't."

"Then you won't mind taking a polygraph?"

"Of course not. Set it up."

"Don't think I won't."

"Go ahead."

"Fine."

Fanny has two boyfriends that give polygraph tests for the Nashville PD. I tell her to call both of them. She does, and within the next 24 hours Dillon takes and passes both tests with—as they say—flying colors, an expression that annoys me. But that's another story.

"Satisfied?" he says.

"No. But at least I believe you."

"Thanks. How nice. I only had to pass two separate lie detector tests to earn your trust."

"Sorry about that."

"No problem. So tell me: where do you think Abbey hid the box?"

"Who cares?"

"You do. It's gonna drive you crazy till I tell you."

"I couldn't care less."

He laughs. "I know you, Dani. You won't be able to sleep tonight. You'll make Sofe so crazy she'll call and beg me to tell her."

"Whatever."

"If you want to know, all you have to do is ask."

I study his face. "Fine. Tell me."

"You admit you don't know?"

"Yes. But only because I haven't taken the time to think about it."

"Would you like a little more time?"

"No."

He smiles. "Ask me nicely."

I sigh. "Dillon. Will you please tell me where Abbey hid the box?"

"Yes." He pauses, then adds, "After you kiss my feet."

"What?"

"If you want to know where she hid the box, you'll have to get on your knees and kiss my feet."

"Fuck you, Dillon!"

"Don't be angry, Dani," he says, imitating my voice. Then he adds: "You know I care about you, don't you?"

"Fuck you!"

"I'm sure you'll figure it out on your own."

"I will, don't worry."

"Good luck with that."

I storm out of his office, go to mine, close the door, put my head in my hands and think as hard as I can. She couldn't have hid the box in her car because Dillon wouldn't have access to it. She couldn't have taken it back to her sorority house, because the police might have obtained a search warrant. She wouldn't have left it with a different friend, because she chose Dillon over all her friends the first time around, which means she couldn't trust any of her friends. Not only that, but why would any of Abbey's friends allow Dillon to open the box?

I ponder all those possibilities and a dozen others, and then call Sofe to see if she has any ideas. She doesn't, so I say, "Turn on your TV."

"Why?"

"Because in the movies, whenever the hero turns on the TV, she sees something that's relevant to the case. Maybe it'll give us an idea."

"You're truly insane. You know that, right?"

"Yup. But turn it on anyway, and tell me what you see."

"You're actually being serious right now?"

"Yes. You're my last hope. It's either that or prepare my lips to pucker up and kiss Dillon's nasty feet."

Sofe turns on the TV, switches from channel to channel, and when she says channel 12 is showing a Red Lobster commercial, it hits me. I thank Sofe, hang up the phone, burst into Dillon's office and announce: "She hid the box in *your* house, under the fish tank!"

"Not even close."

"Liar!"

"She didn't hide it in my house."

"She absolutely did! She put it in the trunk of her car overnight, then drove to your place after you came to work, and put it right back under the fish tank, knowing your home had already been searched. That night, while feeding your fish, you realized the base of your tank wasn't perfectly centered, and you decided to check under the tank before lining it up perfectly, in your OCD way. You don't know *why* you checked under the tank, but you did. And you found the box."

"She never would have put it under the fish tank."

"Why not? It's perfect! The police already checked there."

"Yeah, but then she found out I hide stuff for you under the tank all the time, not to mention you have a key to my house. No offense partner, but she doesn't trust you. She wouldn't have put it there."

He's right.

She wouldn't.

So that leaves only one possible place.

Too bad I don't know what it is.

"Stand, please," I say.

He does, and I look at his feet.

"Will you at least keep your shoes on?"

"That's not how I envisioned it, but...okay."

I sigh, drop to my knees, bend down, and kiss the top of each of his shoes. When I stand back up he says, "She hid it in the hotel room."

"What hotel room?"

"Remember the hotel room I got for her that day? The Hampton Inn? She still had the key, so I assumed she decided to spend the night there. She ordered room service, used the steak knife to cut a long slit under the box spring, and wedged the box inside it."

"How'd you get into the room?"

"It was registered in my name, remember? So just before checkout time I asked the desk clerk if I could keep it another day. He said yes, and I asked for a second key. He gave it to me and I turned the place upside down till I found it."

I think about everything he said. "I'm impressed, Dillon. That was great detective work."

"Better than Great Scott?"

"Probably. Except for the part where you destroyed the evidence."

"Like I said, I wanted to protect her."

"Because you love her."

"That's right."

"You *love* her!"

He frowns, wondering where this is going.

I sing, "Dillon and Abbey, sittin' in a tree—"

He rolls his eyes. "*That's* real mature."

Now I'm giggling and prancing around like I'm six years old, chanting: "K-I-S-S-I—" but stop abruptly when my phone rings, and caller ID shows it's Abbey Rayne.

"To be continued," I tell Dillon, then head to my office to take Abbey's call.

Chapter 12

THERE COMES A TIME in every case...

...where I have to decide if the quirky, unstable person that sat across the desk in our initial interview is smarter than me, hopelessly insane, or both.

Abbey's just smarter than me.

She managed to earn $350,000 in the space of a few weeks. I'm not jealous, I just hope she doesn't get caught. So I start by saying, "Thanks for returning my call."

"No problem. What's up?"

"You lied to me."

"About what?"

"You said your videos were interviews, but they were actual rapes. You also said you didn't have the guts to blackmail the parents, but you blackmailed at least seven of them."

"Sounds like you've been busy."

"Yes. And so has Dillon."

"How *is* Toby?"

"Who?"

"That's what I used to call him. Sweet guy."

"Are you aware he found your box?"

She laughs. "I have no idea what you're talking about, but if he found something I'm not surprised. He's pretty clever."

"You don't sound very concerned."

"Why would I be?"

"The video evidence?"

"Again, I don't know what you mean. But if Dillon found any videos, I'm sure he would have erased them."

"Why would he do that?"

"Because whoever they belong to probably asked him to!"

"When?"

"How would *I* know?"

I think about it. When they were in his house, after the police completed their search, she knew I took the box. She probably asked him to get it back and made him promise to erase all the evidence.

"He loves you," I say.

"I know."

"How'd you make the videos?"

"I have no idea what you're talking about."

"Fine. But let's pretend you suddenly found yourself in possession of a bunch of rape videos."

"Let's pretend some random girl did."

"Fine. Why wouldn't this random girl turn them over to the police?"

"Maybe they were filmed illegally and couldn't be used in court. Maybe she'd rather send them to news outlets in the victims' home towns."

"At least one of the rape videos was taken in the frat house where Tommy Kern was killed."

She says nothing, so I ask, "Why do you suppose the murder video was missing from the laptop?"

"Maybe the girl removed the camera equipment from the basement before that happened."

"Why would she do that? She had a good thing going."

"Maybe she didn't want to get greedy."

"Or maybe she planned to kill Tommy and didn't want the murder recorded."

"This hypothetical girl we're talking about: did she have an alibi?"

"Ironclad."

"Then I'd say she's probably innocent."

"Did you kill Tommy?"

"No."

"Would you be willing to take a polygraph?"

"Sure! If you promise the results will be admissible in court."

"You know it doesn't work that way."

"Then, no."

"Why not?"

"It would serve no purpose."

"It'd help me believe you."

"No offense, Dani, but I don't need your support."

"Does that mean you're okay with me turning the tapes over to the police?"

"I thought you said they'd been destroyed."

"I'm talking about the copies Dillon made."

She laughs. "You're totally bluffing. But if he made copies, then no, I don't think you should turn them over to the police. I think you should send them to the parents of the girls who got raped."

"Why?"

"If you watched a video of your daughter being raped, what would you do to the rapist?"

"Kill him, if I could."

"What would be easier than killing college boys on a college campus?"

"Are you finished?"

"With what?"

"Blackmailing parents?"

"Care to rephrase?"

"Will you promise me right now that you will never—for the rest of your life—blackmail any boy's parents?"

"Yes. Absolutely. You have my word."

"You've lied before."

"True. But how could a girl blackmail someone if Dillon erased all the rape evidence?"

"I don't know. But I'd caution that girl to be happy with what she's already achieved."

"Me too. Can I ask you a question Dani?"

"Of course."

"Why do you hate me?"

"I don't hate you, Abbey. I just didn't appreciate your putting Dillon in a situation where he and I could have lost everything."

"Well, we've already had this discussion, haven't we?"

"We have. But Dillon would never put you in that same situation."

"What do you want me to say? That Dillon's a better person than I am? That's obvious. But you know what? He's a better person than *you* are, too."

"That's almost certainly true," I say. "But the difference is he loves you, and I don't want him to get hurt. And I'll do whatever it takes to protect him."

"Glad to hear it, because I love him too. As a friend, of course. But you can cross me off your list of worries where Dillon's concerned. I doubt our paths will cross again."

"I'm not sure why you think that. Nashville's a very small town. Unless..."

She waits for me to say it: "You've already moved away!"

"The timing's good, don't you think? I'm ready to reinvent myself."

"What about your friends?"

"I'll make new ones."

"And your parents?"

"My mom moved in with her chiropractor, and my dad's a dedicated alcoholic. They don't even know I exist."

"Sorry to hear that. But I hope you come up with a better disguise than the one you showed the Chapmans."

She laughs. "Trust me, I've got that covered."

"Abbey? If this blows up on you for some reason I'll always be just a phone call away."

"Thanks."

"I'm serious. I'm here for you, provided you're 100% honest with me."

"I never lied to you before you told the police about the hitman."

"I know."

"Care to wish me luck?"

"Always. Abbey?"

"Yeah?"

"Dillon's here at the office. Can I put him on the phone? I know he'd love to say goodbye."

"I'd rather not. But if he asks, tell him I miss him already."

"It'll break his heart if he can't say goodbye to you."

"I know. I'm sorry."

"Will you at least call him before you disappear completely?"

"We'll see."

"Sounds like a no."

"It's a no. Goodbye, Dani."

I hang up with a heavy sadness, then head to Dillon's office to tell him about the call.

Chapter 13

"DID SHE ASK TO speak to me?" Dillon asks.

"No. But she *did* say she loves you as a friend and will always miss you."

"You should have put me on the phone."

"Why?"

"So I could say goodbye."

"She'll probably call you at some point."

"I doubt it."

I look at his sorrowful face. "I'm sorry, Dillon."

"You should have put me on the phone."

I can't bear to tell him she refused to talk to him. So I just say, "You're right. I'm sorry."

Dillon's saying something about our friendship needing to be a two-way street, but I've completely tuned him out while reading the text message I just received...and now my heart's sinking faster than the president's approval rating.

The text message is from Callie Carpenter.

She's coming to town and wants to see me. She's giving me nearly two weeks' notice so I'll have plenty of time to block the entire evening for her. Something about a fabulous dinner with a private chef, front row tickets to the Madonna concert, and a suite at the Hermitage Hotel.

Sounds heavenly for three reasons:

1. Callie's the most beautiful woman I've ever seen
2. She's a boatload of fun when she's in a good mood
3. She's the best lover I've ever had

But there are two even better reasons why I don't want to go:

1. I love Sofe
2. Callie's date is scheduled for Friday, November 6th

...The same night I promised Sofe I'd go with her to see her daughter's school play.

What should I do?
What would *you* do?
While Dillon drones on in the background I realize there's only one answer: I have to tell Callie I can't make it. I'll tell her I love Sofe, and can't do this anymore. Can't date her, can't see her. I'll beg her forgiveness, beg her to accept my decision, beg her not to kill Sofe. If worse comes to worse I'll try logic. I'll remind her she occasionally performs

hits for Sofe's uncle, Sal Bonadello. If Callie kills Sofe, it would put a huge strain on her and Sal's relationship.

But the little voice in my brain tells me Callie has zero fear of Uncle Sal, and that she's not going to accept any of my heartfelt pleas. I try to contemplate every possible way our conversation could go, but the overpowering dread remains: I'm almost positive she'll say no.

And if she says no?

If she says no, I'll have to do something even worse: I'll have to call Donovan Creed and ask him to intervene. I'll have to ask him to make sure Callie not only accepts my decision, but allows Sofe to live.

And Creed will do it. He'll solve my problem with Callie. But then I'll have an even bigger problem: I'll owe *him* a favor.

And there are no limits on Creed's favors.

I apologize again, give Dillon a hug, and tell him I need to make a couple of calls.

Now, in my office, I start with Creed. When he answers, I ask: "How long would it take you to get in touch with Callie Carpenter?"

"You mean could I call her right now?"

"Yes."

"Of course."

"Would she take your call even if she were preoccupied?"

"Of course. Why do you ask?"

"I might need a favor."

He laughs. "Don't say that."

"It would be a last resort."

"We've been through this before, Dani, so I won't give you the lecture. Just make sure it's worth it before you ask."

"Understood."

"When will you know?"

"In a few minutes."

I hang up, take a deep breath, then call Callie and start by telling her how much I appreciate her interest, her romantic gestures, and tell her she's the greatest lover I ever had. Then I tell her how I feel about Sofe, and about her having a daughter I didn't know about, and how her daughter's play is on the same day as the date Callie planned for us to be together. Then I tell her I can't continue seeing her, as it wouldn't be fair to Sofe, and Callie listens to all this without saying a word. So I do the whole "I know you said you'd kill Sofe if I ever stopped seeing you, but I know you didn't mean that because you're a good, honest, and fair person, and also because Sal Bonadello is Sophie's uncle, and that would put a strain on your relationship, and..."

"Dani?"

"Yes?"

"Relax."

I ask what that means.

She says, "You want to end things? Fine. They're ended."

"Thank you. But what does that *mean?*"

"It means if you want me to let you go, I'll let you go. You want to be with Sophie? *Be* with Sophie. You want me to promise not to kill Sophie or her daughter? Fine, I'll let them live."

"You promise?"

"Yes."

I let out a huge sigh of relief, even though the idea of killing Sofe's daughter never entered my mind. I thank her profusely, and she says "No problem." Then she drops the bombshell: "Of course, this means you'll owe me a favor. Is that what you want?"

I take a moment to ask myself if I'd rather owe Creed a favor or Callie. And the answer is neither.

Callie says, "If it helps, I already know the favor I plan to ask."

"Actually, that helps a lot."

"Very well. In return for allowing you to break up with me and letting Sophie and her daughter live...you'll have to give me a full week of your time."

I nearly drop my teeth. A whole *week*? How the hell am I gonna swing *that*? What excuse could I *possibly* come up with that Sofe would buy? Because it's not just about my being away for seven days. The part I haven't told you is Callie's number one rule for our time together requires me to surrender my cell phone to her, which means I won't even be able to *communicate* with Sofe for seven days and nights!

Try explaining *that* to Sofe.

On the other hand, if I give Callie this one single week she'll walk away peacefully, and from now on I'll be able to focus my attention 100% on Sofe without having to worry about waking up and finding her severed head in my bed.

"Dani?" Callie says, interrupting my thoughts.

"Yeah?"

"One last thing: our week-long date will begin Friday afternoon, November 6th."

Of course it will.

Fuck.

"You won't regret it, Dani. You're going to have a wonderful time."

"Can we put it off a day?"

"No. Sorry."

"Sofe's gonna be furious if I miss her daughter's play."

"I certainly would be, if I were her."

"She might never forgive me."

"I wouldn't."

"What if she breaks up with me?"

"At least she and her daughter will be alive."

I sigh.

It's always something.

"Fine," I say. "I'll do it."

"Excellent. Be sure to pack your sexiest outfits."

Epilogue

LAUREN CAPSHAW'S LYING ON the bathroom floor, holding her stomach.

No point trying to stand, since within minutes she'll be puking again. A couple weeks ago she felt reborn. As if the weight of the world had been lifted from her. She got away with murder for one simple reason: she didn't give a shit.

For two whole hours life was good. She could finally put her daughter's rape behind her, knowing the bastard who did it was dead.

Then she came home, turned on the TV, and learned she killed the wrong rapist. She'd gone to the frat house, asked for Colson Ford, and the kid said *he* was Colson Ford. She got him to take her to the basement, killed him, and now it turns out he lied. Colson Ford raped Hailey, but Tommy Kern paid for it, which means Colson's still on campus.

He's still a threat to Hailey.

But Lauren has a threat of her own.

An hour ago a young, pale-skinned Muslim lady knocked on her door and said she knew Lauren killed Tommy Kern and could prove it. The lady was wearing large sunglasses and a hijab that covered her hair and shoulders. She spoke excellent English, with a subtle accent that may or may not have been authentic. More importantly, she claimed to have a video of the Tommy Kern murder, and demanded a half-million dollars to keep from turning it over to the police.

Lauren's husband, Matt, went berserk and grabbed the young Muslim lady by the throat and threatened to kill her. But she stood her ground and pointed out she had several accomplices who stood ready to deliver the original video to the police if she wasn't paid by Thursday morning, at ten.

"We know you're good for the money," she said.

Matt said, "We're not going to pay you for something you can't prove. You say you've got a video? Fine. Show it to us."

The girl smiled. "I'll be glad to. But if I show you the video, the price goes to one million dollars."

The End

Personal Message from John Locke:

I love writing books! But what I love even more is hearing from readers. If you enjoyed this or any of my other books it would mean the world to me if you'd click the link below so you can be on my notification list. That way you can receive updates, contests, prizes, and savings of up to 67% on eBooks immediately after publication!

Just access this link: http://www.DonovanCreed.com, and I'll personally thank you for trying my books.

Also, if you get a chance, I hope you'll check out Dani's website:

http://www.DaniRipper.wordpress.com

John Locke

New York Times Best Selling Author

8th Member of the Kindle Million Sales Club

(Members include James Patterson, George R.R. Martin, and Lee Child)

John Locke had 4 of the top 10 eBooks on Amazon/Kindle at the same time, including #1 and #2!

...Had 6 of the top 20 books <u>at the same time</u>!

...Had 8 books in the top 43 <u>at the same time</u>!

...Has written 30 books in five years in <u>six separate genres</u>, <u>All best-sellers</u>!

...Has been published throughout the world in numerous languages by the world's most prestigious publishing houses!

...Winner, Second Act Magazine's Story of the Year!

...Named by Time Magazine as one of the "Stars of the DIY-Publishing Era"

Wall Street Journal: "John Locke (is) transforming the 'book' business"

John Locke

New York Times Best Selling Author
#1 Best Selling Author on Amazon Kindle

Donovan Creed Series:

Lethal People
Lethal Experiment
Saving Rachel
Now & Then
Wish List
A Girl Like You
Vegas Moon
The Love You Crave
Maybe
Callie's Last Dance
Because We Can!
This Means War!
Boxed In!

Emmett Love Series:

Follow the Stone
Don't Poke the Bear
Emmett & Gentry
Goodbye, Enorma
Rag Soup

Dani Ripper Series:

Call Me!
Promise You Won't Tell?
Teacher, Teacher
Don't Tell Presley!
Abbey Rayne

Dr. Gideon Box Series:

Bad Doctor
Box
Outside the Box
Boxed In!

Other:

Kill Jill
Casting Call

Kindle Worlds:

A Kiss for Luck (Kindle Only)

Non-Fiction:

How I sold 1 Million eBooks in 5 Months!

9781942899730

4705ZCB00002B/24
CBHW07184822O626
Chambersburg PA
Lighting Source LLC
www.ingramcontent.com/pod-product-compliance